NOBODY'S DAUGHTER

First Published in Great Britain 2014 by Mirador Publishing

First edition: 2014

A copy of this work is available through the British Library.

ISBN: 978-1-910104-22-4

Mirador Publishing
Mirador
Wearne Lane
Langport
Somerset
TA10 9HB

Nobody's Daughter

By

James Bernard

For Jilly and the Brown Dog

Chapter 1

'What's that noise? It's not their car is it? Look out of the window! Quickly, Joy, quickly. Please, God, it's not them.'

With the strength born of a terrible dread the dying man hauled himself upright on his bed and tried to see the farmyard below. It was not the first time that he had acted thus and his fear was infectious.

'No, Matthew, it's nothing. Only the wind in the firs behind the byre and remember, I've let Lara off her chain. She's bound to bark when they come back, isn't she?'

He sank back into his creased nest of sweaty pillows, the effort visibly hurting him.

'Probably.' And then, with a flash of his former spirit, 'I bloody well would. Heaven knows, she's reason enough.'

The rushed exit from London in response to the urgent secret summons from an anonymous Edinburgh lawyer. The six hours of staring concentration as she drove through the wild December night. A shivering lonely vigil from the opposite hillside until she saw, as she had been told she would, a car leave the house and wind its smoky path away down the valley.

'Forgotten the choke as always,' thought Joy, as unpleasant memory sharpened the reason for her journey.

And all these steps had led here. To this well remembered bedroom, now become death`s ante chamber for the only man she had ever truly loved. Matthew.

She would not cry. She must not cry. Tears were a selfish indulgence she knew. But what a shock!

Two days ago her life had continued its humdrum course, the only variation of note being her increasingly probable divorce.

Now the very hours and minutes counted.

She could almost see his soul sighing and fluttering as it made ready to leave.

Cancer.

All through the lymphatic system. Much, much too late for hope and with no pretence of painlessness.

An overheated room, heavy with the reek of disease. A rumpled bed, sheets grimy from lack of changing. Yesterday's newspapers, wilted petrol station chrysanthemums and a jug of dusty water.

Joy had registered all this with anger and pity when she first opened the door. She had few illusions left about her childhood home and such careless cruelty was not unusual.

It was the fear that was new.

The sense of menace.

A feeling of evil so close and intense that the fine blonde hairs on the back of her hands stood up and her stomach danced a foursome.

She had clung to Matthew in silent compassion when she first came in, trying to lend him some overflow of energy but terror, it seemed, was stronger than love.

'Joy, listen. No, don't talk; we haven't got time. They may come back at any moment and, God knows, they'll butcher you if they find you here.'

His eyes, once so clear, seemed to have plumbed a desperate depth she saw, despite the yellow wash of pain and resignation. But they were still willing her to attention and obedience.

'Go into my dressing room. Be quick. In the cupboard above my hunting kit on the very top shelf you'll find a wooden box. You'll need a chair to stand on.'

Joy removed a quantity of carelessly discarded expensive female attire from the chair in the corner of the room and pulled it over in front of the neatly hung coats and britches. Sure enough at the back of the highest shelf under a pile of old white collarless shirts was a box.

It was old and beautiful. About 18 in. square. Walnut, inlaid with cherry at the edges and a circular silver plate in the centre engraved with a family seal.

'An old silver canteen,' she thought, although judging by its weight, it held other contents now.

Matthew was reaching with slow, painful, movements

into a drawer in his bedside table. The key was still there where he had hidden it long ago.

'Joy Darling, come here. This drawer: pull it out. Right out. Now feel behind. There is a key sello-taped to the bottom left-hand corner of the cabinet. Got it? Good. Pull it away and put it in your pocket. Don't lose it. There isn't a spare.'

It was, she realised, the first time that he had relaxed since she had arrived.

'Sit down, Darling. There's a story that I must tell you. The best sort of story because it's true and the proof is in that box. But we haven't got much time.'

It seemed that, in fact, they had no time. The dogs had started to bark.

Matthew became instantly infected with the panic that is companion to physical disablement and mental despair.

'Go. Go. Take the back stairs. Run. No; you must go now. What can they do to me ? The only thing left to them is to hurt you. I know you love me; so go.'

And now Joy was crying. She hugged the man who had been her childhood idol. Her touchstone. Proof that good was stronger than bad. But bad had seen her car and with angry shouts was thundering through the hall towards the staircase.

A last heart destroying kiss, but his terror gripped her.

'The box, Joy. For God's sake don't let them get the box.'

They were the last words she ever heard him speak. The beseeching tone of his voice echoed down the drab years of her childhood. But fear would not let her stay.

'It's that Turnbull bitch. I thought it looked like her common little car.'

'Andrea,' thought Joy. 'I should be able to dodge her.'

'I'll catch the little thief. She'll be on the servant's side. I'll bloody well kill her.'

The authentic voice of Petronella in reply. A different obstacle altogether and one that now blocked the foot of the stairs, scarlet and spitting with hate.

'I knew it. She's stolen something. Hurry up. Come and help me.'

Joy felt her feet being kicked out from under her and

3

heard, rather than saw, an etiolated fist narrowly miss her face, making instead impressive contact with the oak door frame.

She used the resulting howl to get up and run.

Andrea was coming the other way, a pair of bellows above her head. They collided and Joy felt the bellows smash down on her shoulder.

She went down again.

Petronella had sufficiently recovered to resume the chase and now hurled herself on Joy, sweating, swearing and grasping for the box.

Down came the bellows again.

Alas for the home team! They hit Petronella's head, not the intended target. Joy scrambled to her feet, flung the front door open and sprinted for her car. The harpies were behind her but God had evidently had enough.

With a ferocious snarl, Lara the Alsatian leaped at Petronella, biting her hard on the shin; something she had looked forward to for some time. Petronella stayed down. Lara then turned to Andrea, holding her at bay, her wrinkled lip and bared teeth leaving no doubt as to her intention.

Joy had always been her favourite.

The car started first time, her luck was holding, and Joy fled; the precious box safely on the seat beside her. She risked a last look up at the old grey house.

The condemned man had hobbled to his bedroom window. He raised his hand and, although it could hardly be, she would later swear that he seemed to be laughing.

Chapter 2

Joy sat in the garden and basked. It was a glorious day. The immediate chores were done, the rest could wait. Above all it was quiet.

Apart from the background hum of insects busy with the last of the lavender and circular bed of white roses, the only noise came from the lazy movement of sheep cropping the grass in the field across the lake from where she dozed.

Her family were all occupied with their own schemes and away.

Her husband at some long winded meeting until, at least, the evening. Her two children at their respective universities.

It was, for once, just her and the dogs lying and twitching with their dreams in the sun.

Joy too was almost asleep but her dreams were less benign. She was reliving her childhood.

This had happened quite often in the past few weeks; ever since a girlfriend, whose daily reading consisted almost entirely of the court and social pages, had innocently announced that Andrea was dead.

Memories. Gladdies, the Dumfriesshire hill farm that had been the backdrop to her infancy and adolescence. Lonely and lovely, hidden at the head of a steep winding valley.

The old house and steading shielded with firs and framed by heather purple hills.

The clear little streams that fed the hidden loch. The fat flat hay meadows by the burn that wound down all the way to the far river Nith.

Andrea dead. It was not really a shock and certainly not a cause for sorrow.

All her life Andrea had complained of ailments both real and imaginary. Evidently, this time, she had not been making it up.

Their last two meetings were impossible to forget. She had tried.

The first, a physical affair. Assault with curses for dialogue. She shuddered. The second, almost nothing.

They had hardly looked at each other at Matthew's funeral. Spoken not at all. Then parted forever.

Both had been dressed in black but despite outward appearance there had only been one real mourner.

Tears had always been Andrea's forte. Tears, Joy thought, always tears. Tears to hide untruths discovered and tears to keep yet other lies buried.

She had known for as long as she was able to remember that Andrea disliked her.

From the perspective of her sunny garden she could now accept this. There had been no real reason why she should have been liked.

But where had the bitter hatred come from?

After all, she thought, she had been just a little girl. Mrs. Turnbull's child. The cooks daughter. No threat to the Andrea, the lady of the house. Matthew's wife.

Beautiful and grand. Cold and calculating. Pleased only by the mirror and the small expensive boxes that her husband offered up in periodic exchange for peace.

A mad insecure, insatiable jealousy to find threat in the smile of a six-year-old.

Then there had been Matthew's daughters. Andrea's two little princesses. Much worshipped, less often loved.

Petronella, a year younger than Joy. Charming when it was useful, otherwise petulant and entirely devoid of conscience.

Elsa, three years younger. Shy, overawed by her sister and largely ignored by her mother.

It was largely due to Petronella's ceaseless complaints over Joy's status in the house that she was sent away to boarding school at the age of only seven.

The childish snobbery and clever lies still hurt almost 40 years on.

'Mother, why must we share a governess with Joy? The Murrays don't share with their groom's son and Serena Cowen says that she's dirty and we might catch something off her.'

Or,

'Mother, do we have to go in the same car as Joy? Johnny Laidlaw says it's common to travel with the servant's children and anyway she smells of sheep.'

There were many others in the same vein and any breakage, deliberate or otherwise, saw Joy accused.

A climax had to come. Its name was Wedgewood. An entire tea service.

'Joy. Leave your silly pony book and come and look at this. It's very old and valuable so you mustn't touch it.'

Petronella opened the glass-fronted cabinet in the drawing room. The translucent quality of the porcelain was obvious. It was beautiful.

She should have expected the sudden, determined shove from behind. She was learning to be wary of Petronella. Not wary enough.

With a terrible, expensive, snapping and cracking, the glass shelf into which Joy had cannoned fell, raining its precious contents onto the three lower tiers causing them too to collapse.

A moment's horrified silence, an icy stare of power, and Petronella started to scream.

The outcome was never in doubt.

Joy stirred. Time for a cup of tea, but the memories were not so easily appeased.

The Cedars non denominational school for girls in Edinburgh was as dry and unfriendly as the name itself.

Joy, thanks to Petronella, had learned little from the governess and found herself lagging behind her fellow pupils. Nonetheless, here she could be herself. Taken on her own merits. A social equal.

With hindsight, she recognised the start of what her husband called her stubborn streak. She had needed it to survive. Without it, she would not be in this garden now.

The Cedars prized silent self sufficiency. Joy learnt quickly. She survived the mundane school day dramas. They were trivial compared to the Gladdies gestapo.

She was not expelled; she even thrived.

7

The end came when Andrea discovered who was paying school fees. Not being given to insight, she had not thought to question how a cook could afford such luxury.

More tears, Joy remembered. Tears with two results.

The first, an immediate move to the local village school. She was not even allowed to finish the term.

The second; a red Jaguar convertible. Evidently the tariff for a resumption of what passed for peace in their marriage.

A smile. She had loved the village school. Home every evening, spoilt by her mother and loved by the dogs and pet lambs.

Then, with a frown, another puzzle. Equality with Matthew's daughters.

The benefactor had been Matthew's mother and the philanthropy that comes with rich old age. All three girls were quietly but firmly in rolled in Path head Castle School, that old ladies Alma mater.

The dogs could sense the relaxation in their mistress as she strolled idly round the garden. Her thoughts were happier.

Having children of her own, Joy could see the irony of this next stage in her life.

That admirable old lady had believed in education as the surest path to a woman's independence.

Path head had been, at the turn-of-the-century, a shining beacon of female emancipation. When Joy arrived times had moved on but unfortunately neither curriculum nor teaching methods had kept pace.

A genteel stagnation had taken root. Sport and music were strong points but the girls who went on to take A-levels with any degree of success were rare indeed.

This did not worry Andrea who often grandly declared that all the girls needed in life was piano, French and ability on a horse.

Odd, since she was proficient in none of these three disciplines herself.

Joy flourished in this antique environment. It was true, she admitted, that she did not possess much in the way of paper certificates as a result. But she had met girls with backgrounds even more peculiar than her own. They did not seem to pay much heed to their circumstances, so neither would she.

Armed with this social stiffening, she was sent out into the world aged 16.

She could ride, play tennis and the piano. She could not speak French. In fact, she could now see that she had been totally unqualified. Perhaps girl groom?

It had not seemed so then.

This unfortunate fact, acknowledged by Mrs Turnbull, was ignored by both Matthew and his mother.

The girl had been to Path head. Therefore she was educated. It could not be otherwise.

Despite these firm convictions, it had proved rather harder to convince prospective employers. They, tiresomely, insisted on proof.

Moreover, she had never liked Edinburgh. Still didn't. It was now a question of taste. Back then, her social status had shut many doors.

There had been one other overriding problem. Despite denials then and now, Joy was pretty.

Prettier than Matthew's daughters. More engaging. More fun. In short, more in demand.

This was a situation which Andrea could not tolerate. It was made worse by the wry amusement with which Matthew teased her at home.

Perhaps age had lent her perspective, but even then, Matthew for once, seemed not to care.

If Andrea was blind to this subtle change in her husband, Maud ,her mother, was not.

Matthew was vital to Maud's plans. She had never saved anything, spent with abandon and Matthew was her only consistent source of income.

Her lender of last resort. Her healthcare. Her pension.

His extraordinary affection for the cook's daughter risked diluting this fund. A solution must be found.

It was also a puzzle. Why did Matthew seem to care so much for this girl?

To mind as twisted as that of Maud there were several

possibilities, all rooted in sex; but without certitude she could hardly blackmail and despite diligent research in the salons of Edinburgh she was no further forward.

The girl would have to go.

Maud had contacts in the Glasgow Italian diaspora. She could have hardly foreseen the long-term consequences.

Milan, Joy thought happily, as she dead headed the roses. It had been as beautiful as the job was dull.

She had been that social 'must' for a certain class of Italian; the British nanny.

True, she lacked certificates, references or indeed experience. The price however, was too good to quibble and Maud had assured the family that Joy adored cooking, cleaning and ironing.

Her first job. Not really anything, yet everything. A door to a new life.

Milan started a still enduring love affair with Italy.

The job itself was not hard. The child was unpleasant and its parents argumentative but time off was heaven.

While she loved Scotland, its urban architecture could not compare. Nor could its climate. Cold rain does not encourage the leisurely exploration of little streets and squares.

It was however the interior of these beautiful buildings that made the greatest impression. The word 'fresco' entered her vocabulary and the vibrancy of what she saw stunned her.

It still did.

Six months flew by and she returned home. The problem of her presence had been delayed not solved.

This time Andrea and Maud took no chances. Mrs Turnbull was advised that she could make occasional visits, not more.

It was the second step on the journey that led to this sunlit garden with its lengthening evening shadows.

'Why did he care?'She wondered. 'Why risk another bout of matrimonial anarchy for me?'

Perhaps the precious box that he had bequeathed her and she still cherished held the answer. But its secrets were in a code indecipherable to her. Its meaning long since buried, along with its former owner, in the cold Scottish soil.

And now it seemed, the vault was to be re-opened.

She had recently received warnings that the past was not forgotten. Two e-mails from separate and trusted sources spoke of a stirring of interest in her. For the box had held another treasure, one comprehensible to all and its absence had been finally noted.

The hunt was up. She was the quarry and her persecutors those modern-day huntsmen.

Lawyers.

Chapter 3

Haunting warnings. Two of them. E-mails from a far-off country and an evil, buried past.

At first Joy had tried to ignore them, hoping that like a black thundercloud on a summer evening, they might pass, taking their destructive power elsewhere.

And it had been such an evening.

A beautiful evening, a time to be outside, to mow lawns, attack brambles and get horses fit for hunting.

Her children were gone, even the lambs had been sold and a reluctant husband been bent to the mundane tasks of farm maintenance.

None of these facts excused Joy's careless disregard of her computer but, in truth, she had never really joined the electronic age.

It was also true that the spot where she lived had neither broadband or 3G wireless signal.

This meant that getting connected was a painfully slow business requiring time and patience.

Joy had plenty of the former but the latter had never been a strong point.

The immediacy of the telephone was more to her taste.

It had been therefore some time before she had noticed the two messages hidden between thick layers of routine adverts and special offers.

She recognised the authors of those messages at once. Neither were regular correspondents.

Johnny could be relied on for the occasional joke or an annual round-up of Scottish gossip usually at Christmas.

Spender was less regular, indeed his offerings were normally requests for bed, slander, or both.

The Internet connection was particularly slow that day and by the time she had read a girlfriend's chain letter she had had enough.

She knew the messages were there but considered them

unlikely to be important. In any case Spender, at least, could ring if he really needed to talk.

It seemed that he did.

That evening the answer phone had one message. It was succinct.

'You are incredibly hopeless. Go and read your emails and ring me tomorrow.'

No name, but the voice was unmistakable and the tone authentic.

Joy was only moderately intrigued. She and Spender went back a long way.

A considerate manner was reserved for those occasions when he felt bruised. This, evidently, was not one of them.

He would ring again if he deemed it sufficiently important and she had a dinner to cook.

The message next morning was even more abrupt.

'Read your messages. Mine and Laidlaw's. Read them now.'

With a prickle of disquiet Joy rang Spender.

No reply, but this was not unusual. With a heavy heart she sat in front of her computer and composed herself to wait.

Now she knew.

The past had not died with Matthew or her mother or even Andrea.

It was astir once more, driven by Petronella's fury and she could hardly vanish again. She had her own family now.

She would have to fight.

Chapter 4

A cold tentacle of air curled around his hands as John M. Joffrey sighed and shut his bedroom window. He was a small greying man, somewhat ruffled at the edges like a solicitor who has seen too much of the chaos of everyday life.

He was, he had, and he felt uneasy.

Despite the street lights it was almost dark with a thick Edinburgh haar making of each one its own small yellow island. Driving to and back from the dinner tonight would be slow and boring, as probably, would be the dinner itself.

But this was no ordinary evening. It was the annual dinner of the High Constables and Guard of Honour of Holyrood House, an elite body of thirty men trusted with, in the Captain of the Guards tortured prose, 'the security of the capital's Palace when royal personages were present.'

At least, thought Joffrey, none were present tonight and the Captain would have no reason to shout and look angry. Indeed, this was supposed to be a relaxed, almost family, affair. Albeit in white tie and with a total absence of women.

However, in Joffrey's experience, much of what took place had been already decided, if not ordered, by the various spouses. He, for example, had been told to discover what Mrs Mabel Cunningham and her flock of lady followers were planning to buy for Mrs Joffrey's 65th birthday present so that she could look suitably surprised without running the risk of actual surprise.

He loved his wife dearly but apprehensively and would try. Perhaps, he thought, it could even be incorporated as some light humour into the main event of the evening; his speech.

For John M. Joffrey was not a simple guest, nor even a run of the mill constable, after thirty five years he was the Moderator, and this was his night.

Holyrood could be felt as a looming, cliff like, presence through the mist as he parked his car, noticing with satisfaction that not too many were ahead of him.

There had been a time, he was embarrassed to admit, when the Constables were better known for their attachment to large gin and tonics than their glorious 800 year history and any event like this had been guaranteed an early start.

Putting his keys into his pocket he felt again the tug of his evening tailcoat. It had been an early burst of pride that had led him to the door of Curtley, the smart tailor, some thirty years ago but now he regretted the impulse. He would have been better to hire, as his wife had pointed out. At least his clothes could have grown with him. He sighed again and despite the pull of the coat, squared his shoulders and walked into the quadrangle.

Not far away, on the doorstep of the New Club, Sir Merlin Hayley bt. also sighed as he climbed into his taxi. Unlike John M. Joffrey this was not the result of ill fitting clothes or his wife's demands. He also had a speech to deliver, being the guest of the Moderator.

He wondered again why he had accepted Joffrey's invitation, but consoled himself with the thought of the morrow on the River Tweed and perhaps, some duck fighting to follow. This, he thought, would be with real old friends and no damn Edinburgh etiquette.

Sir Merlin was a proud man, small and trim, latterly a Member of Parliament for the West Country and still, he felt, a reasonably lionised QC. Now head of his chambers, despite the best efforts of his clerk, he was a man who commanded respect from doormen and taxi drivers alike.

He was not disturbed in his thoughts as the cab groped its way through the murk towards Holyrood.

This gave him time again to ponder the cautiously worded request for a confidential meeting the next day.' Edinburgh discretion,' he thought sarcastically, but perhaps he could prise something out of Joffrey tonight.

They had first met, he remembered, more than fifteen years ago at some useless symposium on company law both North and South of the border.

It had taken place in the unlikely neutral venue of Leeds. He had taken to the frankness of Joffrey as opposed to the quietly superior air of his Edinburgh colleagues, and also, it had to be admitted to a mutual readiness to adjourn to the type of bar that served alcohol rather than briefs.

An occasional friendship had been the result and this was not his first dinner at Holyrood. The memory of food and wine cheered him slightly despite the fog and odour of stale chips in the taxi. He too squared his shoulders and braced himself for the evening ahead.

By two in the morning both men were holding glasses in the Constables Mess across the courtyard from the Palace. They were alone, this being the moderator's right, despite the liquid insinuations of several less senior members.

The dinner had followed the usual ritual, tolerable food, better wine and the unique and delightful pause for lemon sorbet and black Sobranie cigarettes as a palate cleaner between fish and meat.

The speeches had been made, Joffrey's long and anodyne, Hayley's short and not too rude. In any case both had been applauded and immediately forgotten.

Now, with whiskey and tobacco each man pondered the as yet unspoken business of tomorrow and wondered who would first broach the subject.

Chapter 5

The next morning found Edinburgh a different place. The haar had cleared to low, fast moving, puffs of cumulus and the view across the Firth into Fife was impressive over the rooftops of the old town.

At least this was how Sir Merlin consoled himself as he descended Frederick Street to the offices of Don, McCluskey and Younger W. S. where Joffrey was senior partner.

He had declined all Sir Merlin's probing the night before, claiming that clear heads were called for, and perhaps, Sir Merlin admitted to himself, he had been right.

In any event the air was doing him good and with luck he would be away and on the river by midday.

He was slightly surprised to find the offices, apart from a very proper and very Morningside, receptionist deserted.

However, a bustling and purposeful Joffrey soon greeted him with no sign of the post dinner malaise that he still felt behind his eyes.

Joffrey's office was as sparse as he remembered, with no personal touch or indeed, any clue as to his character or even, outside of the law, interests.

Sir Merlin, by contrast, liked to remind his clients just how lucky they were to have secured his services, and why they must pay such enormous fees, with a careful selection of photographs, certificates and other paraphernalia charting his social and professional progress.

Coffee was decided on and arrived with a slim file all balanced on a battered tray and, with a final disapproving look, the receptionist retired to guard her desk. And so it began.

At first, Joffrey reiterated the need for discretion. That there were well-known people involved. That the press would leap at the news and scandal would surely result. This Sir Merlin, who was privy to most of D. M. Y.'s client list, sincerely doubted, but with rising impatience bided his time.

Meanwhile, Joffrey, like a diner unsure of a menu, was taking furtive peaks at his file. Silence descended until Sir Merlin could bear it no longer and gently, or so he supposed, asked,

'But what John is in there,' pointing at the file, 'and how am I or my chambers concerned?'

This seemed to rouse Joffrey from his introspection and with a sad smile he said,

'The root of all evil Merlin. Enough for us both.'

The story began not long after the war and, as with many good stories, opened with hope and high expectation.

A young man, a demobbed soldier was at the start of his peacetime civilian life. He had been gravely wounded at Arnhem with the ill fated first British airborne division.

There had followed months in hospital and many more in rehabilitation. The problem was with his back and legs and there was doubt, not only over the prospect of ever walking again but also, at times, with his life itself. Joffrey paused,

'As you will have probably surmised, Merlin, this young man became a client of mine and latterly a friend. A good friend. His name by the way was,' and here he paused.

'Well, Matthew will suffice for the moment.'

'However,' as Joffrey continued, 'slowly doctor time, along with the new antibiotic wonder drug, penicillin, had worked its wonders.

Septicaemia had been, narrowly, defeated. The legs were saved and muscles painfully rebuilt.

More importantly, the constant reminder, in the beds along the ward, that others were not so lucky had stiffened the mind.

Self pity, he knew, is not conducive to healing.

Moreover, Matthew had a dream and this did not involve offices, desks and chairs. He would be a farmer.'

'Luckily, in terms of financial wherewithal, this was not for him as for so many others, a pipe dream. Matthew, or rather his family, was rich.'

'Not rich,' Joffrey hastened to explain, 'in the fashion of financial plutocrats or footballers, but solidly, worthily, Scottishly well off. More than comfortable.'

'Whiskey or coal mines,' thought Sir Merlin to himself.

'Jute in Dundee,' Joffrey confirmed. 'Earlier generations had been rather too partial to the turf and private trains. Nonetheless, Matthew's father, a very senior retired soldier could afford in those days to indulge a favourite son, but on condition that he first learn his job.

For Matthew there followed a year at the Royal Agricultural College in Cirencester where to his father's surprise he gained an approving report, although as he later discovered, this had had as much to do with the number of days following hounds as work.

'His professor was a hunting man.'

'Next was a year high on the West Coast as a gentleman shepherd to a man himself not quite a gentleman.

It was the terrible winter of 1947 when the snow came and stayed, Hinds had to be shot in their hundreds or starve and only the fittest ewes survived.

'Matthew survived, even prospered though he was never paid.' Joffrey allowed himself a smile, 'they had I am told, a sideline in breeding terriers for rich women. There was, seemingly, a dearth after the war.'

'God help us,' thought Sir Merlin.

'The promised reward for this period came in the form of a farm, bought in the ring at Lockerbie market, along with the livestock and implements to furnish it.

It was not a large farm nor was the house imposing but it was in the heart of the hill country near Dalton and very beautiful.'

'Didn't have a beat the Annan did it?' asked Sir Merlin, startled into wakefulness by mention of the great outdoors and the receding prospect of his own fishing.

'Bear with me Merlin, it is a story worth the telling you will find, and, ultimately, you are involved.' Which only added to Sir Merlin's discomfort.

'With the farm came hunting and, as ever with hunting, came sex. What was more unusual was that here sex turned into love.'

Sir Merlin was now paying more attention, sex often meant offspring, money had already been hinted at, and in his experience, love meant passion, passion meant litigation and litigation meant fees.

'At first all seemed well. The girl, let us call her Alice' said Joffrey, 'despite coming from south of the border, was of good family and with excellent prospects.

She was the only child of a passive mother and doting but overbearing father who, as is often the case with controlling parents, had too little to do. He had been the lucky recipient of a textile fortune and credited himself with the industry and insight not always evident to others.

The parents met once and it was not a disaster. They had some mutual if distant friends and soundings out revealed no skeletons.

An engagement was announced and a wedding date discussed.

Matthew had been accepted into the semi-feudal class of Dumfriesshire society which largely revolved around hunting. All agreed that Alice would be an asset, if only to act as a restraining influence at hunt balls.

The house was tidied and at his mother's suggestion, it was agreed to find a housekeeper. An advertisement was duly placed in Horse and Hound eccentrically for a woman and border collie, with the proviso that both must be good workers'.

They arrived on the same day.

The collie was not a success.'

'The same was not true of Mrs Turnbull. Strictly speaking she was Miss Turnbull but it was thought better for all concerned that she should be married.

Even a fictitious husband generated less local scandal than would have been the case otherwise.

In any event, Mrs Turnbull precluded gossip. I remember her well.

It was said that she came from the East Coast. She was certainly taciturn, even dour and sufficiently plain to be proper.

Behind this off putting facade was a kind, well educated woman. She had been a theatre nurse during the war and had seen much.

She adored horses, could ride, cook, manage a budget and help when needed during the lambing.

Her only drawback was a fondness for the bottle, although this was not much remarked upon in a valley where every farm had its own alcoholic.'

'As the wedding drew closer Alice's father became ever more busy, concerning himself with all aspects of her future life.

High on his list was her new home to which he had been invited by Matthew twice but each time refused.

Suddenly it became imperative that he make an inspection and he duly arrived without his wife and intent on trouble.

Nothing was right. It was too small, too isolated, the drive was too rough, the housekeeper not sufficiently respectful. There were far too many dogs. In short it would not do.

His daughter could not possibly live there and be happy, despite what she said and if a wedding was to take place, all must change.' Joffrey paused,

'He must have been a very difficult man because Gladdies, the farm, was and is beautiful. A Scottish Shangri-La. A hidden valley of burn, loch and brae. Ringed by heather and earthworks as old as the hills themselves.'

Joffrey looked up, embarrassed by his own oratory.

'Well it is. In my opinion, he simply could not bear to let her go and would have found any excuse to prevent it.'

Both men nodded, both were powerful in their own world and power is an addiction which takes discipline to master.

Sadly for Matthew and Alice her father had never known discipline and, in the 1950s, independence among young girls was not as common as it is today.

'The result was inevitable. Despite the tears and pleading, the engagement was broken. Both their lives became darker places.

For Alice this was particularly so. She had not told Matthew, she could not tell her own mother, but she was pregnant and very frightened.

In the end, and as unlikely as it may seem, she turned to Matthew's mother. They had not been particularly close but

Matthew's mother was fond of Alice and knew that she had made her son happy.

She was also a formidable woman, a hangover from an earlier age and, after what seemed a lifetime married to the military, used to dealing with self important men.'

'Nothing was said to either father and Alice was quickly dispatched to Switzerland to stay with 'friends' and mend a broken heart.

Her father, for once, agreed; being somewhat in awe of Matthew's mother and happy that his daughter would be far from Scotland.'

'I am not privy to the precise details,' Joffrey continued, 'but in any event a baby girl was born and given up for adoption.

This, Merlin, is where I need your help.

I believe it to be the case that you are professionally acquainted with the parents of the orphan's mother.

Moreover, that there having been no further issue and barring other intentions any legacy involved would logically devolve upon this child.'

This woke Sir Merlin from his reverie as he struggled to translate Joffrey's convoluted statement into plain English.

As always, caution was his immediate instinct, especially as he thought he discerned something akin to emotion in Joffrey.

'Two points occur to me John,' he replied.

'First, I would like to know why you assume that I may act for this family.

Secondly, I shall require much more detail to even begin enquiries. A name for instance?'

He had spoken more sternly than he intended and was surprised to see a quiet smile light on Joffrey's face.

'You don't deny it then? And you do have an unresolved testament?'

This provoked an immediate reaction and considerable bluster from Sir Merlin as had been the intention.

For, it was true, there was one case which would have been unremarkable save for the complexity involved.

It had been the recent basis of several spurious claims, much unprofitable work and embarrassing interviews. It seemed, however, impossible to him that the solution lay here in Scotland.

'Do you know this girl, woman, this ex-orphan? Is she your client?'

'Sadly I do not. 'Was the reply 'and forgive me for burdening you with further detail but it is germane and you will, I think, see my dilemma.'

Sir Merlin had no choice but to acquiesce and settled with more or less good grace to the renewal of the story.

The child, Joffrey said, had been given away.

This as he had much later learned from Matthew was not quite true and again, the moving force had been his mother.

'She was, even then, a quite elderly lady, used to getting her own way either openly or by subterfuge. Importantly she had no grandchildren. She was, I am told, very family minded.

In any case she fixed it between herself and Mrs Turnbull and only after the event informed her husband and son.'

And seeing the look of disbelief continued,

'Yes, Merlin, there was an immaculate conception at Gladdies and with Mrs Turnbull's forbidding mien, caution overcame curiosity. It was a fact and a private fact.

What did Matthew and, for that matter, Alice say?

What was their reaction you ask?'

Sir Merlin had not asked; he had begun to suspect something along these lines but it seemed churlish to mention this when Joffrey was so obviously enjoying himself as the flourish of his normally cautious hands showed.

'Matthew was, by his own account, shocked, overjoyed and bewildered.

Alice was never told and never knew. His mother insisted and he loved and respected her.

He also told me that she mentioned considerable financial implications if he broke silence and, as I am sure you are aware, fox hunting and sheep farming are uneasy companions from the revenue standpoint.'

'Gladdies , therefore, was now a house of three. Matthew, Mrs Turnbull and the blonde baby girl, Joy Turnbull.'

'I take it that this is not her real name since you have so easily divulged it?' Sir Merlin asked with a touch of sarcasm.

He was rewarded with,

'That, I'm afraid, I do not know.' A long pause. Despite himself Sir Merlin was intrigued and a little shamefacedly, after his bout of temper, asked Joffrey to continue.

It was here, Joffrey said that the story took an ugly turn.

'Matthew, as has happened before to jilted men, suddenly found himself the object of intense curiosity. Moreover, being available and somewhat vulnerable, much scheming.'

Before long a tryst had been contrived by a Glasgow lady who Joffrey, showing real feeling, described as 'wicked'.

Matthew had no defence. 'The daughter was beautiful, headstrong and seemed to his eyes, very sophisticated.

In fact her mother was the sophisticated party, in that she knew exactly how and when to apply pressure.

Matthew buckled.

On the rebound, he became engaged again.'

'This time there was less love. There were furious arguments, passionate reconciliations and a lot of tears but Matthew persisted.

His parents, even his father, warned him that he was taking on not only a girl but an entire family.

All to no avail.

Even a particularly vile tantrum when they received a wedding present from Alice could not dissuade him.

He must have had doubts but they were private and repressed.

Perhaps sensing this, his future mother-in-law hurried proceedings and Matthew and Andrea were duly married in St.Vincents, Glasgow and thence to the south of Italy on honeymoon.'

Here, Joffrey seeing Sir Merlin's impatience quickened his pace.

He explained that the marriage had, not without difficulty, endured. Matthew had fathered two further daughters and despite Andrea's constant hostility and incomprehension, treated Joy as if she were his own.

He knew that, for the moment anyway, he could not tell Andrea the truth. She was already bitterly jealous and utterly incapable of discretion.

'Thanks to Andrea, Joy's education was short. She left school at sixteen, had various jobs and because Matthew, for once, insisted, took a secretarial course at Cambridge.'

Joffrey did not know all the details.

He did know, because he had been there, that she had been married from home to an older man and that the relationship had not lasted.

Shortly after this wedding Mrs Turnbull, her liver a wreck, had died.

This was the first blow for Joy but she still had Matthew. They had always been close said Joffrey.

Thus, when Matthew contracted a cancer they became closer still. The end sadly was not long delayed.

Matthew, weakened by a vindictive wife and grasping family in law, died.

He was buried in the graveyard of the local church where Joy had been married at a small family service.'

Joffrey stopped and rubbed his eyes.

'Joy vanished , there was nothing left to hold her and she went. I have no idea where she is.

No idea whether Matthew ever told her or Andrea the truth. But I think not.

I do not even know her name.

A search under both her married name and that of Miss Joy Turnbull has revealed nothing and her two sisters either do not know or will not tell.'

Sir Merlin privately favoured the latter option.

Money, as he had frequently observed, is more often a solvent than glue where families are concerned.

Joffrey continued, finishing his story,

'And yet I must find her, I owe it to Matthew.

Some assets were left in trust to her on Andrea's death. She is now dead.

As I think I mentioned, the sum is not inconsiderable.

Frankly, Merlin, I am at a loss and, forgive me for being direct, I believe that your business mentioned earlier might help. It is a legacy that you are trying to place is it not?'

Sir Merlin took stock.

He realised that he could not nor should, prevaricate any longer.

He was surprised and disconcerted that Joffrey should know so much of the nature of his business but perhaps the whole saga of this troublesome trust could be finally closed.

He decided to cooperate.

'John your intelligence is excellent, I congratulate you. One day you must tell me how you do it.

In answer to your question, yes, it is Alice Playfair's Will Trust that you refer to. However, as are you, I am without the beneficiary.

Tell me, your trust; discretionary?'

A nod.

'I thought so. And the trustees?'

A shake.

'The clock cannot run for ever, how much time do we have?'

Joffrey, gladdened by the 'we' relaxed.

'Enough. I cannot stall ever but, I hope, long enough.'

With that the meeting drew to an end.

It was agreed to an initial exchange of information by letter followed by a further meeting if and when detail had been uncovered.

Sir Merlin would use his contacts in London and they were many, now that he had perhaps, a name.

Joffrey would tackle the Scottish end and, in particular, Dumfriesshire.

He had, of course, already tried but recounting the story had hardened his resolve.

It was perhaps also relevant that he had not been fully open with Sir Merlin.

Matthew, it was true, had n been a close friend.

He had liked and admired the man.

Much more importantly, he knew and loathed Andrea's family.

For him, a sense of vengeance for Matthew was the spur.

Chapter 6

Joffrey replaced the Edinburgh telephone handset back in its cradle with a slight smile; the exasperation in Sir Merlin's voice had been so thick as to be almost tangible.

'If you spent as much time tracing her as you appear to do following me you'd have found that wretched girl by now.'

In London there was not even the memory of a smile on Sir Merlin's face as he considered Joffrey's request.

He had jotted down the details. 'The Wiltshire Secretarial College in Cambridge and the Our Lady of the Fens Convent. Did they keep records? An old girl's newsletter perhaps?'

Indeed any information at all on past students. Especially a Miss. Joy Turnbull.

It was, needless to say, a logical favour to ask and the effort required, minimal. He began to calm down while remaining piqued at the cavalier fashion with which the clerk's office disclosed his movements.

Joffrey was correct, he would be in Cambridge shortly for the annual dinner of the Westminster College Miscreants society and a small deed to ask, in essence one question, was not a great hardship.

In the normal way of things Sir Merlin did not attend the Miscreant's dinner.

He was not particularly proud of his old college nor had he ever been an oarsman of renown.

For a while, after coming down, he had kept in touch and even made an annual donation to the boat club. This modest insurance had not, however, paid out and none of his children had been offered a place at Westminster.

It was therefore with some surprise that the secretary of the Miscreants had received the application for a ticket to the annual dinner.

It was well-known that Sir Merlin would have preferred Trinity and, in social terms, regarded Westminster as little more than a boarding house for Northern Grammar School boys and long-haired theology students.

In several respects this was an accurate appraisal.

However, the passage of years had moulded Sir Merlin's memory to fit his many prejudices.

Westminster had indeed been a college with a northern bias which accounted for its annual success in rugby Cuppers but it was also among the foremost in law.

A Senior Tutor after Sir Merlin's time had been an unusually far sighted man.

An eminent professor of law, he was intimately involved with the governance of several great public schools and did not share in his colleagues' academic disdain, snobbery really, for the mundane subject that was college finance.

He and the bursar dug away until they had exposed the void that was college future financial planning.

Creditors were legion and no one had deemed it necessary to think ahead.

Intellectually, this was considered vulgar; they would muddle through, they always had and in any case the University would not let them sink.

For the Senior Tutor this was simply lazy; he understood the rich and knew the value of appearance.

Accordingly a new type of Westminster undergraduate began to appear. They were never very many but they all shared a common thread.

They were large, they were rich, they spoke what, to a Cambridge man, is laughably called Oxford English, they may not have been terribly intelligent but they could row.

In a few short years Westminster had progressed steadily up the Cam; the boards in the Goldie boathouse began to record Westminster among the colleges of those gilded few and a reputation was born.

It is not, perhaps well understood that people aspire to Cambridge for things other than academic excellence and the subsequent doors that open.

To a select few, rowing is religion, an end in itself.

Westminster could not, of course, survive on the head

ship of the Cam alone. The Senate House would not tolerate it and in any case, this was not the Senior Tutors aim.

The plan soon began to bear fruit.

Westminster became, perhaps for the only time in its life, fashionable.

The Senior Tutor could pick and choose more widely, with the endowments of recent old boys allowing a judicious leavening of the mix with some really bright scholarship students.

It was thus that the college came through its own black hole. There had been enough first class degrees, just, to avoid censure.

The deficits had been made good and the coffers filled.

Fashion is a fickle thing and Westminster could not be an exception to this rule. Gradually the public schoolboys became rarer, the Boat Club slipped gently down the river and there were less empty fire extinguishers and broken panes of glass after Bumps Suppers.

It was to this fading era that Sir Merlin came to dine.

Westminster had not been his first choice and his acceptance of the offered place had astonished his father, a Trinity man, possessed in full measure of that colleges complacent conceit.

Sir Merlin, while no scholar, was not stupid and realised that he owed his place more to his families Far Eastern trading connections then any single exam result.

It would have been a more than normally rabid Senior Tutor who could have not found a place for the scion of a commercial dynasty. It was simply sensible and usually paid dividends.

Sir Merlin had lived and socialised elsewhere.

Apart from fishing and shooting he had always avoided sport but deigned to row in a lowly summer boat for the Mays.

This had really been the sum total of his engagement with Westminster as an undergraduate but, in the years since, he had watched the clever state schoolboys rise to position and power in the city.

Some were even members of the same St. James's Street clubs as him.

For many the passage of time is a social ointment, smoothing rough and sharp edges alike.

This was not the case with Sir Merlin; if anything, his stint as an MP had only fuelled his sense of self worth and, despite their evident merit, he regarded these new men as upstarts, parvenus.

They had had a generic name for these types when he was up he recalled; they were NARGs, not a real gentleman, and so they remained to him still.

For Sir Merlin, accent, attire and ancestry spelt the value of a man. Ability came lower on his private list.

Nonetheless, they were often useful and touchingly keen to help an alumni of their old college.

So with the hypocrisy that came naturally to him, Sir Merlin was ready to flatter and use them.

It was, he thought, the only reason for attending the Miscreants dinner.

It was information rather than sustenance or good company that he sought and for information one sometimes had to make sacrifices.

As can happen, although not often in Sir Merlin's experience, information came from an unexpected quarter.

On arriving at Cambridge he had kept the appointment made for him by Joffrey with the Mother Superior of the 'Our Lady of the Fens Convent' which also ran a profitable sideline in accommodation for young girls.

These latter tended to be A level retakes or aspiring secretaries. Girls from good families but not of under-graduate grade.

The rooms were sparse, even spartan, the food poor and facilities, apart from an ancient laundry room, non-existent.

Accordingly the fees were vast and waiting-list long.

It was here that Joy had been lodged by Matthew's mother on arrival in Cambridge and, given the Mother Superiors refusal to discuss former inmates, either on the telephone or by letter, it was here that Sir Merlin came.

The interview had been abrupt to the point of rudeness.

No, the Mother Superior had no current details of Joy.

Had she, she would not divulge them without Joys express

permission and, in any event, she had no recollection of any Joy ever lodging there.

As a last, and he supposed, futile appeal Sir Merlin hinted at a legacy.

He noted the sudden gleam in the eyes opposite.

The Mother Superior was not as unworldly as she seemed and like everyone else, had rates and other expenses to pay.

However, no further details were forthcoming and Sir Merlin left this curious female establishment.

He was not to know that the Mother Superior had not been entirely truthful.

She did indeed remember Joy.

One does not easily forget the only girl ever expelled from the convent in almost thirty years.

Joy had not been really bad, she recalled; no drugs, no drink.

Cigarettes, always cigarettes she thought, as she lit one herself.

Cigarettes and boys.

Nice boys to be sure, but rules were rules and after several warnings the final discovery of a young Scotsman from a family well-known for its wildness hiding behind the washing machine, Joy had had to go.

The mother Superior had missed her but Joy had not seemed duly upset and the man Matthew who paid the bills, even less so, talking happily of economies.

She had had no further news of Joy and so, she considered, she had not really been untruthful, merely discrete.

The Wiltshire Secretarial College was even less helpful.

Only the brass nameplate remained, alongside the 'For Sale' placard.

For Sir Merlin the information came later in an after dinner alcoholic fug of reminiscence and 'whatever became of so and so?'

He had not really been part of the conversation and his motives for attaching himself to a group many years his junior was not altruistic.

They were the new generation of financial mechanics; mergers and acquisitions their trade.

What remained of the old Hayley Far Eastern trading house was rumoured to be in play with obvious ramifications for Sir Merlin and his family.

One of the group, a large man and ex-Blue was very senior in the American firm rumoured to be behind the manoeuvring.

Sir Merlin, who had not divulged his surname, was counting on Kummel induced indiscretions. In particular, names for the various counter parties, to date only hinted at in the press.

In this he was to be disappointed.

One does not become a senior partner in a hardnosed American outfit by accident. However, in passing, Joys name came up.

At first Sir Merlin paid no heed. He was, in fact, hardly listening, merely nodding his head and silently reflecting on the gold vulgarity of the Halls new paint scheme.

It had, he reflected, cost a fortune as he had cause to know, having received an endless collection of begging letters.

Westminster had never been known for its taste,' But what could one expect with a natural sciences professor as Master', he thought?

His group of young financial princes were laughing.

Unlike Sir Merlin they had contributed to the re-decoration and were ruefully commenting on what their money had bought.

One in particular, was giving vent to his feelings. He knew, or rather used to know, he said some girl, a rag roller or suchlike who could have done a better job for a fraction of the price in less than half the time.

Surely they remembered her?

'The blonde girl for heaven's sake. The one that old Mick was forever mooning about.

The one that Sporran had claimed was his girlfriend.

What was her name? It began with a J or perhaps G. June, Gail, Julie? No, I remember now; Joy. Scottish girl, blonde, bubbly, always up for a party. Expelled from the convent. Wonder what happened to her?'

'More to the point' asked another voice

'Where the fuck are Sporran and Mick? They never come to these things. Bloody public schoolboys they're all the same.'

This with a sideways glance at Sir Merlin who inclined his head in acknowledgement.

The conversation moved on, increasingly raucous, with the drunken re- telling of favourite anecdotes.

That yob who had driven his battered Jaguar into the college quadrangle only to be repelled by a hail of beer glasses.

The time Sporran had filled the sump of the Boat Club van with water and the radiator with oil.

Sir Merlin stifled a yawn, it was late, these young men were not of his generation and he was obviously not going to get any further with the question of the Hayley takeover.

However, as a sop to Joffrey, he would make enquiries tomorrow with the College Secretary.

He brightened, he might even unearth some nugget with which to bait his Edinburgh colleague.

Sporran, Mick and in particular Joy.

They had been up at the same time as his party of fellow diners and thus he had approximate dates.

Nicknames should present no problem for the elephantine memory of the Porters Lodge.

His room was as uncomfortable as he remembered.

The walls were scarred with ancient blue- tack, the carpet stained with something more sinister.

The windows nailed shut and the clanking radiator on a roasting and un-stoppable power.

However, daylight eventually came and the end of nocturnal torment.

Breakfast was in the same hall as last night's dinner, miraculously cleared by staff the college hired from the local asylum, claiming charity but with one eye on the tax benefit also.

The smell of wine lingered mixed with bacon and coffee;

if he shut his eyes Sir Merlin could almost imagine himself taking the three am. breakfast at some provincial hunt ball.

The Secretary was brisk and helpful. She personally, did not recall the surnames behind Sporran and Mick but a quick call to the Porters Lodge produced the information. Laidlaw and Bouleau respectively. Both had been oarsmen of the noisier type.

'What other type was there?' wondered Sir Merlin.

Laidlaw, thought the porter, had got his Blue. Bouleau not.

The secretary confirmed that neither had shone academically although they had managed to graduate.

Despite the erstwhile Senior Tutor and his plan for financial sustainability, neither had yielded up much tribute, not even to the Boat Club.

Yes, she had an address for Laidlaw but it was Hong Kong pre-1997 so probably out of date.

As for the other, he had disappeared and despite appeals in the annual college magazine no one seemed to have heard of him.

He had, she thought, been going abroad but that was all that she could say.

Chapter 7

For Johnny Laidlaw it had been a Monday morning much like any other.

He was a tall wiry man, physically strong, good looking in a slightly dangerous way and boasting a healthy Borders' complexion, due in equal parts to weather and whiskey.

In short, a Laidlaw of the same stamp as those who had plagued the English down the centuries with their reiving and cattle rustling.

His lifestyle too would have resonated with his ancestors.

He was, by profession, a farmer. By passion, a foxhunter and always, by day or night, a playboy.

This was not to belittle him for Johnny had never been arrogant, was hardly ever intentionally rude. Amusing rather than aggressive when in his cups.

His particular peccadillo was the fair sex; he adored women and was, mainly, adored in return.

There was only one complication to this hobby; distance; the Borders are sparsely populated at best. Johnny was therefore obliged to travel and his battered pickup and evil smelling lurcher were well-known to anxious mothers and their delighted daughters from Inverness to Exeter.

He went by many nicknames. The travelling dog fox. Tom cat in a dressing gown, and since he was an MFH, the more astute, 'must find heiress'.

All were, to some extent, accurate.

Farming does not provide the revenue stream it used to, while fox hunting has not become noticeably cheaper.

Certainly Johnny had private means, thanks to a series of judicious marriages by the male line ,but the turf and, latterly, Lloyds had taken their toll and a half share in a pack of foxhounds requires money on an almost Homeric scale.

It was therefore with a sense of anticipation that he re read the letter from Don, McCluskey and Younger signed by a Mr John M. Joffrey W. S. whom he did not know.

Johnny was by nature an optimist. For him there were two types of lawyer's letter.

Threats from outraged paterfamilias, with which he was, sadly, well acquainted; and bills.

This was neither.

Rather, it was an invitation to get in touch by letter or even telephone, which was almost risque for an Edinburgh lawyer.

A meeting was required.

This meeting could be at a venue of Johnny's choosing, but on the whole, thought the writer, his offices in Edinburgh would be the prudent and discreet choice.

The subject matter was only shyly alluded to;

'To discuss a matter germane to this partnership and to yourself.'

For Johnny's money, and he sincerely hoped that it would turn out to be his money, this was dividend time.

It had happened before, some half remembered spinster cousin leaving him a house in Leicestershire quite out of the blue.

It had been a case of, as Joffrey would have had it,

'as the good book says, to those who have, more shall be given.'

The anticipation of a windfall to come gave Johnny an appetite even for the ill-prepared offerings that passed for lunch with his housekeeper Mrs Donoghue.

This did not engender the surprise that it might have done.

Mrs Donoghue was in the habit of perusing Johnny's mail and having seen his letter, could well understand the impatience to make a two o'clock telephone call to Edinburgh. With satisfaction she listened from the pantry to the placing of the call and the fixing of an appointment.

It was, she noted, to be held here in the Borders, the following week.

This she understood.

Johnny hated suits and ties.

More importantly, he knew the advantage of home ground where, he hoped, the initiative would be his.

While Johnny awaited the meeting with something approaching complacency, this was not the case with Joffrey.

He believed in being prepared as well as was possible and, after decades of experience, had caught the eager edge to Johnny's voice on the telephone, knew what it meant and realised that in the disappointment following the declaration of his real business a certain truculence was to be expected.

It would have been easier, he knew, to unveil his questions in a letter beforehand, the better for Johnny to answer them.

However, his research showed that discretion was not always Johnny's strong suite and Joffrey feared the reaction of Joy's half sisters if they learned that a lawyer was looking for her.

He realised, of course, that in the end a bloodbath was inevitable but wished to stall hostilities until any arrangements were considerably more advanced.

Johnny Laidlaw he learned, had been born in 1959, the second child and only son of the hon. John Laidlaw deceased and Iona Laidlaw (née Carnegie) also now departed.

He had been brought up in the house in which he still lived and, for a time, shared the same governess as Joy and her sisters.

It had been a muscular type of childhood, Joffrey realised.

An authoritarian father, artistic mother and nanny who had only eyes for his sister, meant that any affection that he had experienced came from dogs or ponies.

Joffrey was no psychiatrist, indeed had no time for them, but even he could see that this might be at the root of Johnny's present lifestyle.

Things had not improved with age.

The result of constant reprimands and public humiliation had been a shyness bordering on autism.

This, noted Joffrey, seemed to have been only a temporary state of affairs and no one could now accuse Johnny Laidlaw of timidity.

In any case, the boy to his father's disgust, had failed his common entrance examination for Eton and been subsequently sent to Forres.

'Ah,' thought Joffrey, himself a Watsonian, 'Forres for polish.'

It was where he had sent his own son but the age difference meant that they would have not coincided.

Further enquiries had revealed a not unexpected sticky start.

A short period of bullying, almost de rigueur in those days, had come to an abrupt end with the onset of puberty; the beginnings of an adult Laidlaw physique.

Although a now attractive man, as a youth he had been too ungainly and, intermittently, spotty to attract the attention of those older boys who were either over sexed or uncertain of their proclivities in that direction.

The usual progression had followed.

The normal rites of passage, cigarettes and alcohol; something Joffrey noted that seemed to have been only temporarily abandoned, and resumed with enthusiasm when the discipline of school was over.

The saving grace, as is often the case with country boys, was sport.

This was not unexpected given his pedigree.

What was unusual was that this had been accompanied by an academic calming and a settling to his books. He had not been brilliant. No school prizes came his way but he had worked consistently and was rewarded with O and A level results that had pleased his tutors and astonished his father.

These, when added to his prowess on the rugby field, had suggested that Oxbridge was not out of the question.

To be sure, the college would have to be carefully chosen and perhaps some debts called in, but in those days Scottish schools were not exactly overrun with Oxbridge alumni and any chance, however slight, was something to be seized.

The downside was small, disappointed parents protesting an extra term's fees, but in the event of success, much trumpeting and a useful edge over the rest of the pack north of the border in the cut throat world of public school recruitment.

The search had not been as complicated, nor the need for tact, as great as the Headmaster had feared.

Westminster's drive for financial security and the means being used to attain that end, were hardly a secret to those whose business it was to know these things.

Indeed, had they been, they could hardly have worked.

Understated publicity requires a world class brand to succeed and Westminster College suffered no delusion in that area.

Johnny stayed the extra term, sat the Cambridge papers for geography and was duly called for an interview.

At his father's insistence a new suit was purchased and he was carefully rehearsed in that old despot's view of world affairs.

Luckily for Johnny this had been anticipated by his tutors and both clothing and opinions were duely modified to accommodate Westminster's current, contradictory, mood.

Thus Johnny found himself on the London Sleeper wearing clean but slightly shabby corduroy trousers and an inoffensive tweed jacket.

There had been debate about ties.

In the event it would not have mattered, but the Scottish Rugby Union colours were finally considered sufficiently neutral and a subliminal reminder that he had been called for the National youth team trials might prove helpful.

Unbeknown to Forres there was no need for this angst.

The Senior Tutor at Westminster knew what he wanted and Johnny fit the bill.

A well-connected and old family, adequate academic results, sporting potential and, here he admitted to himself, the thrill of the gamble, a hope of future public school loyalty which led to endowments, unexpected donations and that ultimate goal, a lasting social cachet.

Johnny, therefore, already had one foot in the ring.

As long as he was not more than normally gauche he could hardly fail.

He was not; nor did he.

A gap year had followed. He had matured and hardened in the unforgiving world of an Australian jackaroo.

His natural affinity with both horses and alcohol had

helped and although not exactly liked, he had earned a grudging respect from his fellow farmhands despite being that object of Aussie derision, a pom.

Cambridge had come as something of a shock.

The work was hard, there was plenty of it, and most alarmingly he was required to think for himself, develop opinions that were reasoned, not just received or the result of personal prejudice.

The hardest blow, however, had come with the College and University Rugby Clubs.

There appeared to be few enough kindred spirits at Westminster anyway and those that existed had, to a man, decamped to the Boat Club.

His fellow rugby players, while undoubtedly capable, sported alarming amounts of facial hair, had thick north country accents and wore nylon clothing of the type not usually associated with the Brideshead dream.

At the Boat Club, on the other hand, he could relax to the familiar public school bray, high jinks, fire extinguishers, broken glass and comfortably right wing opinion.

Johnny learned to row.

It was no surprise that he was good at it. He was naturally athletic and his eye for a ball gave him the poise appreciated in a boat. He was not clumsy as are most apprentices.

To the surprise and it has to be said, jealousy, of his more exalted counterparts, he quickly became a fixture in the College Eight and began to attract the attention of the Goldie Boat Club.

This elite does not usually bother itself with novices. There is always talent enough to be sifted and measured from established sources and little enough time to choose and weld together a new crew for the spring encounter with Oxford.

Luckily for Cambridge they had Alf Sin.

Alf was the University Boatman, charged with the maintenance of the Goldie boathouse, upkeep and rigging of the racing shells and, just occasionally as a sideline, some coaching.

He was not one of the fashionable modern coaches, bought in as an alternating stream pandering to the whims and tastes of the current president, but a constant and steadying element; a tradition in human shape.

There are certain underlying truths to the art of rowing that no amount of tinkering at the edges can change.

Of these, Alf had over thirty years' experience.

Accordingly, those hopefuls who had put themselves forward for University trials and felt themselves to be wanting after harsh criticism from the modern men, would turn to him as to a guru.

He never disappointed. His style was abrupt, usually rude but always pertinent. It was here, Joffrey learned, that Johnny had acquired the unoriginal, for a Scotsman, nickname of Sporran.

He had turned to Alf, along with others, for some fine tuning and the hope of redemption from the President and his entourage.

There had been a tall Etonian, 'Long John Silver', a middling Etonian, 'Nothing at all', and a short Etonian, 'Umpty dumpty', among the seekers after truth.

All had failed.

Perhaps they were too conditioned by past coaching. Johnny was not and a seat in Goldie, the reserve eight, was the result.

They won comfortably that spring where the Blue Boat failed and the contribution made by the number six oar was duly noted.

Johnny never looked back.

His star in the sporting firmament fixed, he could afford to relax a little and devote more time to the serious business of fun.

The annual Tripos exams were a nuisance, occasioning several scares, but the Senior Tutor was a pragmatic man; separated his Firsts from his Blues and dealt accordingly.

It was with this question of leisure, or in any event parties, that Joffrey decided to start.

He had motored down to Jedburgh after putting his office juniors to work and intended to arrive at Kirkstiel, the

Laidlaw seat, in time to transact the bulk of his business before the lunch to which he had been invited.

He was in no doubt that Johnny expected a bearer of glad tidings and knew from past experience that the first few minutes of any exploratory mission, such as he was engaged on, were crucial.

He did not know Johnny personally although his research had provided a wealth of detail and plenty of colour.

He was not, therefore, overly surprised by the man who opened the front door and strode across the gravel to meet him.

He was taller than he had, for some reason, imagined.

The handshake was firm.

An overall impression of vitality and openness. He did not look or act his fifty two years.

As different, thought Joffrey, as possible from those similarly aged young men in Edinburgh whose attempts at gravitas only resulted in a grey monochrome.

This was, perhaps, not a fair comparison. Johnny, while not born with a golden spoon in his mouth, certainly had considerable advantages over his fellow men in both physique and inheritance.

Acres in sufficient quantity lend a certain confidence to even the shyest or least prepossessing of men and Johnny was neither.

They settled, after the usual discussion of road and weather, in Johnny's study.

It was a large room, the walls covered with yellowing Hessian and photographs of long dead military men, horses and dogs.

The desk was at the far end under a window with a view to distract all but the most dedicated.

Judging by the confusion of paper everywhere, Johnny did not count among their ranks. Various terriers and a large and shaggy lurcher were ejected fondly from the available chairs and coffee was brought by one of plainest and, thought Joffrey, dirtiest looking women he had seen for a long time.

He did not, however, fail to note the keen gleam of

interest in her eye and knew his guess concerning Johnnies expectations for the meeting to be well founded.

Several long moments passed as Joffrey opened a battered brown briefcase, arranged the contents to his liking, adjusted his half-moon spectacles and cleared his throat. The opening, when it came, seemed to Johnny promising.

'As we discussed on the telephone, I am here on business of a rather delicate sort and before I divulge the subject matter I would ask for your promise of confidentiality. At least for the present.'

Johnny readily agreed and lent forward.

At last the meat.

'The affair in question concerns you only in the most indirect fashion but I would be extremely grateful for any help you may be able to give. I am, frankly, in a bit of a bind at present.'

At the other side of the desk there was an almost imperceptible slumping of shoulders, a lessening of vigilance.

Johnny was still prepared to hope but even allowing for the legendary reticence of Joffrey's firm this did not sound to him like the preamble of fortune.

'I have trying, for some time now, to establish the whereabouts of a young woman who I believe to be a friend, or in any event, acquaintance of yours.

It is imperative that I contact her.

Time is pressing and she seems, intentionally or otherwise, to have vanished.

I am speaking of the erstwhile Miss Joy Turnbull latterly of Gladdies, Dumfriesshire but possibly now married and certainly elsewhere.'

The question asked, Joffrey looked up apologetically and was met with a long and penetrating stare.

'He knows', he thought, 'but will he tell?'

Chapter 8

Joy Turnbull. Once met not easily forgotten.

Yes, Johnny knew Joy.

One does not share a childhood and forget.

One does not hunt, dance reels, drink and he admitted, for his part, imagine something deeper, without indelible memories.

They had, from infancy and well into adolescence, been close. Welded together by a sense of outsidership, not totally belonging.

Johnny, the result of a Victorian upbringing and Joy the Victorian morals that then prevailed.

Sex, despite his best efforts, had been avoided and as a result the friendship was deeper and certainly less complicated than was the case with most of Johnny's female acquaintances.

There had been a pause when Joy, abruptly, left school but then, to his immense surprise, she had emerged, as a butterfly from its chrysalis, at Cambridge.

In theory, he remembered, she was learning to type.

He doubted whether this was money that had been well spent because, in practice, she was everywhere but the classroom.

Thinking back, he was hard put to recall a party where hadn't seen her.

Blonde noisy and above all fun, she had been the subject matter of many male dreams beside his own.

Sadly, for the frustrated undergraduate community, her affections had been elsewhere. Somehow or other she had met the mature man, an object of much speculation and deep mistrust to the hedonistic teenagers who supposed themselves an elite.

The mature man was untouchable and un-knowable, a superior being, military, of the red and blue clan. A Guards officer.

That this lordly individual had been smitten did not astonish Johnny but his patience did.

Joy was not easy to control.

To no one's surprise, least of all Joy's, typing had not been a success.

Jobs had been relatively easy to find, harder to retain.

Johnny, meanwhile, had been recruited by an eminent firm of establishment bankers on the strength of his ability with the oar, was based in the city and saw as much of Joy as anyone.

While the boyfriend toiled, as the military must, in the discomfort of Windsor and Knightsbridge, Joy continued to read for her degree in the university of life.

Johnny had lived some of her many adventures at second hand, usually in Plavios, a jolly but fake Italian establishment off the Kings Road.

He remembered the stint at MacDonald's in Earls Court and Matthew's gratification that she was working for an American multi- national. She had hidden behind the deep fat fryers, he recalled, when he had paid a visit.

Then there had been the Directors Lunches incident.

Joy had telephoned Mrs Turnbull for her egg and prawn recipe.

A fire had resulted followed by the usual dismissal.

More successful had been the foray into the rag trade.

This was the 80s, the era of the gilded city boy. Striped shirts and loud braces.

Joy had called in her Cambridge contacts, cycled to the Square Mile and charmed entire trading floors with verbal flannel and shirt samples.

It had been one of rare examples of good taste resulting from greed.

Nothing lasts forever and her shirts had not worn out fast enough.

Under increasing threat of an engagement ring, combined with wanderlust, Joy cut and ran.

Johnny had been sad to lose her but he too was moving on. His particular brand of capitalism was more suited to Asian rules and Hong Kong called.

He had, again, to thank the light blue Mafia for his introduction.

Oarsman may not always be intellectuals but their contacts are hard to beat.

One of the great China trading houses was his new home and among his many onerous tasks, the delightful chore of selecting air hostesses for the associated airline.

Johnny was in his element.

Joy had paid him a visit some months into his tenure.

She was spending her shirt profit in company with a girlfriend from Cambridge days, travelling in India and the Far East.

Hong Kong was not really on their itinerary but the chance of a hot bath and a few American Express lunches, his card he remembered, had been too good to question.

Their adventures had been legion but funds were limited and lotus eating could not be indefinite.

The military boyfriend had cornered her in Bali for a fortnight and, she admitted, she missed him just sufficiently to make Britain not seem impossible.

True, he had not been as robust as the Australian backpackers she had met. Despite his stories of Army hardship he had utterly refused to stay in her usual losman accommodation for more than one night.

Blankets and long drops were not, apparently, his thing.

So she had come home, resigned to the pressure she knew would follow.

Johnny remembered the marriage vividly.

For the inside observer there was much to note.

It had been that peculiarly Dumfriesshire type of December afternoon.

Overcast, a mixture of drizzle and snow falling, yet luminous in the way only a hill country can be.

He had taken his annual leave to coincide with the wedding and his intuition that Joy might need a shoulder close at hand had not been wrong.

Andrea had excelled.

Exceeded even her own high standard of spleen, indeed become Shakespearean in her torment.

The problem had started with Joy's simple wish to be married from Gladdies.

Matthew had been delighted.

The year before he had had to pay for Petronella's nuptials.

St Mungo's Cathedral and The Inverness. The outlay had been enormous, both to the Episcopalian church and to the hoteliers.

Andrea had been in her element, her ghastly family much to the fore and there had been an eclectic collection of superannuated Glasgow playboys as guests.

The cognoscenti from Dumfriesshire had looked on with pity and quiet distain. It had all been really rather vulgar and, by the end, even Andrea had perhaps had some inkling of this.

In any event she did her best to delay, frustrate and complicate arrangements. Johnny well recalled the list of objections.

Above all, she was the cook's girl. Gladdies was not her home. She must pay the going rate.

Besides. There was nowhere to site the marquee. Despite the obvious untruth of this claim, the garden was declared too small.

Two. The caterers and wine merchants would refuse to deliver to such a remote location.

Three. The church was tiny and dull.

Here Andrea ignored her previous claim that no one would come to a housekeeper's daughter's wedding; such an ostentatious display of wealth would appal the locals.

They, in the event, were thrilled to be invited and all came.

Then there was Joy herself. What was she to wear?

Mrs Turnbull and Matthew were ready for, and capable of dealing with this final straw but Andrea was not to be denied.

Many things were said in the three week run up to that day that were worse, much worse, than what had ever gone before.

The full depths of Andrea's jealousy, insecurity and stupidity were exposed to the entire family and anyone else who happened to be present.

Some, such as Petronella and Andrea's mother, Maud, were approving but their reasons were venal rather than noble.

As for Joy, her resolve hardened.

The only surprise was the depth of dislike that had been revealed. Not the fact of it. Matthew's education and upbringing obliged him to treat everyone with the same courtesy irrespective of social class.

He had often explained to his children that, Duke or Dustbin man, one's manners remained identical.

Andrea came from a different tradition entirely.

Here, weak and lowly were of little consequence save that from time to time they might be useful.

It need hardly be said that this attitude was not a winning one in a world of shepherds and tractor men.

In any event, no dress was forthcoming, or indeed any other accoutrement.

Joy painted a pair of shoes cream, cut a ruinously expensive but nonetheless discarded dress in half and matched the bottom with a self sown top.

Needless to say, when that fact was revealed months later, Andrea, who had not recognised her own dress at the wedding, suddenly developed a quite extraordinary attachment to it.

The only item that marked Joy out as being more than a housekeeper's daughter was a very large diamond broach that Matthew, in a fit of daring, lent to her for the occasion.

Andrea was to make him pay dearly for this bravery in the months to come but it still gave him great satisfaction.

The wedding itself had been great fun, remembered Johnny.

At Joy's insistence he had been made an Usher and had watched in amusement the military hierarchy with its associated mores at the Usher's lunch.

From the various stories recounted he was glad to have missed the stag night which had taken place in London one month earlier.

The military guard of honour made up of senior NCOs, resplendent in their State Uniform, had been magnificent and the men themselves, even more so.

There is a reason why Britain often prevails in war.

Men like these are it.

The service was rousing and mercifully short. The Kirk full to overflowing and the reception superb.

Andrea had not entertained the idea of dinner or dancing so all in the marquee were under pressure to extract an evening's worth of fun and gossip in just three short hours. This was not ideal given the distance most had travelled, but the resulting compression made for noise.

The speeches had been, all things considered, reasonable and again, sensibly short.

The not quite Godfather who, by his own initiative, was also leaving piper, gave a typically eccentric offering. Incomprehensible to all but himself and then retired.

The Best man funny, not vulgar and remarkably free of military jargon and in house jokes.

The groom sober and slightly nervous which was understandable given the witches coven of Grandmother, Andrea and Petronella just to his left below the dais.

Johnny could also remember the emotion he felt as Joy left for her honeymoon. This had not been unexpected but was as nothing to the tears on Matthew's face, or the open grief expressed in the bristly and alcoholic hug of Mrs Turnbull.

Since then his meetings with Joy had been increasingly few and had now ceased.

Yes, there had a honeymoon after which the newly weds had installed themselves in some drab military married quarters in London.

The soldier then continued blithely on his pre-designated Army path and had assumed that Joy would conform with the expected norms of the military caste.

Sadly, for him, this would not happen.

Partly it was his own fault, but it was also the inevitable and long overdue clash of two different worlds.

The Victorian ideal of duty and the late 20th century dogma of entitlement.

In the first place it seemed astonishing, even to the

unimaginative mind of Johnny, to expect Joy to change simply because of a gold band on her finger.

Indeed, if he thought back, he could not remember her ever wearing one.

Plenty of other rings certainly, but not the conventionally accepted insignia of wedlock. Surely, he thought, the Soldier must have anticipated some kicking at the traces and factored into his plans a period of gradual immersion?

Joy, after all, had not exactly raced to the altar and that very wilfulness that first attracted him must have engendered some expectation of dissent?

Apparently not.

It came as a profound shock to the Soldier.

Joy did not fit and would not mould to his preconceived ideal of an army officer's wife. It did not matter that this perfect being did not in fact exist and that if he had looked even slightly harder this would have been evident.

The fact that Joy insisted on having her own career; just then taking form as an idea; hated the petty regulations that govern the furnishing of military accommodation and evinced no interest whatsoever in the activities of the Regimental wives club astonished him.

For a week or so he regarded these failings with a benign eye. Then increasingly, less so. Quickly what, to him, began as a quirk became a challenge.

Army officers are brought up on challenges.

From the initial officer selection board, through Sandhurst and, if one is clever enough, which he was not, Staff College.

War itself is the ultimate challenge.

To some extent army officers are self selecting. This means that they must already possess, to a large degree, those characteristics which the military will then develop.

A tendency to give up easily, surrender, is vigorously suppressed or, more usually, detected early and, reasonably from the Army's viewpoint, used as grounds for rejection. This is not to say that a mulish stubbornness is praised.

Rather, a determination to succeed: in army parlance to achieve the aim, allied to the intelligence and cunning to get there by, if necessary a circuitous route, is the goal.

Sadly, this was not the Soldier's way.

It was also, incidentally, why he had failed his Staff College exams.

He came from an earlier generation of British officers which knew only frontal assault. The old nursery maxim of 'if at once you don't succeed try, try, try again' was his watchword and like some First War general, each setback was met with a new assault accompanied by increasing levels of force.

That the Soldier was like this was not entirely his own fault.

Any organisation is only as good as its current occupants.

Things have changed today but this was the 1980s and Joy was, arguably, ahead of her time.

Like many other girls she had been seduced by good looks, athleticism and the easy but superficial charm of that type unique to courtiers, diplomats and the better regiments. While she had proved susceptible in the short term she was too independent to remain hypnotised for long.

It was an uneven match.

The Soldier was used to obedience from below and loyalty to those above. It had not occurred to him that marriage might not follow the same rules.

Certainly his mother, a cowed and dull woman, had never openly questioned his father's dictates and now encouraged him in his quest for subjugation.

He became by degrees frustrated and increasingly angry at Joy's resistance.

There was also an undercurrent of, not to be admitted, shame at this impotence. If he could not command his own household, how then his men?

The teasing of his colleagues only hardened his resolve and an unhappy stalemate was the result. The final straw had been the inevitable posting to Germany.

Joy had, by this time, embarked on what was to prove a lasting and lucrative love: paint. She was not to be budged. She argued, logically, that other wives were not following the drum and the melodramatic predictions of military sanction for the husband were unfounded.

Harder for the Soldier to gainsay was the fact that Joy now earned more than him, with the prospect of greater things to come.

London was in the grip of one of its periodic love affairs with decorative paint effects. Joy, with increasing expertise, could supply this and was much in demand.

She had, with the last of her dwindling resources and the proceeds of returned wedding presents, put herself through three months of school.

Here she had learned, at the feet of one of the better contemporary exponents, the dark arts of faux marble, wood graining and various other effects.

Her fellow students had been mainly young girls of that class which must kill time between school and marriage. Daddy was paying and no one was marking the result.

For Joy it was different.

Not only did she enjoy her studies, she was good, and had seen in Italy where they could ultimately lead.

It felt right, and after graduation, her bank manager could only agree.

Her not quite sister, Elsa, had already gone down this road, albeit from a different starting point and they joined forces, bringing each other in on their various jobs.

Their clients were many and varied; from American impresarios, the best payers, to members of the Royal Household, the worst.

An increasingly impressive CV and growing portfolio was the result and lead to people prepared to wait.

It was against this background that the Soldier departed, alone, to Germany.

It was not a good parting.

The tears were acrimonious rather than tender and future plans very uncertain. In a more prosaic vein, Joy had again to find somewhere to live.

After a couple of rather squalid bedrooms in unmarried girlfriend's houses, the answer to her problems came at a noisy and impromptu drinks party in Fulham.

At that time Fulham was still affordable and had been

largely colonised by that now almost extinct breed, the Sloan Ranger.

Joy was painting what was, to her eyes, a vulgar and over the top, marble panelled bathroom for a well paid young stockbroker she had met in her shirt selling days.

It was a Friday evening and he had arrived home early after what he described as a 'Bolly lunch' determined to continue the party.

Telephone calls had been made, a dash to Endbins, and people had started to appear, among them, as he well remembered, himself.

Johnny had, in the two or so years since Joy's wedding, been sent back to London.

This was only partially due to the increasing number of complaints from eminent Hong Kong fathers.

Potential loss of business aside, his employers thought that he might profit from a less licentious atmosphere and London office know how.

He had taken the call towards the end of a dull Friday afternoon, been tempted by the list of his co invitees and persuaded by the fact that Joy was already there.

He had not bothered to go home and change, simply hailed a taxi, removed his tie and made for a well-known nautical Chelsea pub where he was sure to find friends. He was not disappointed.

Among the noisy crowd, standing out by his poise as much as his height, was his old companion from Cambridge rowing days, Saville Spender.

They greeted each other warmly and despite the lack of a specific invitation, Spender needed little effort to be persuaded that his presence at the party of a man whom he hardly knew, but nonetheless often derided, would be appreciated.

A taxi was summoned by an imperious hand, Johnny gave directions in the full knowledge that this doomed him to paying, and they left.

Spender was one of those individuals to whom the term 'exceptional' was not an exaggeration.

He was exceptionally large in every way possible.

Physically, this was not unexpected in an oarsman, long levers allied to big muscles are the recipe for boat speed. Less common in the species is a keen intellect and an even sharper wit.

He had begun to mellow somewhat, but as a younger man modesty had not been his forte. As he himself, from time to time, stated, he had little to be modest about.

This was said in a charming self deprecating way, but no listener ever really believed that he meant it.

He was, inevitably, an Old Etonian and seemed to have followed a golden road through life.

There was no doubting his academic ability despite a certain lack of paper certificates. This was not his fault

Quite by chance a murmuring appendix, later proved to be just that, had unfairly robbed him of the chance to shine at A level.

Predicted grades and aquatic ability carried him to Cambridge.

Unkind tongues spoke of a Spender library which indeed later appeared, but no definitive link was ever proved.

Whatever the truth, Spender was Cambridge's gain.

His star ascended quickly and shone bright.

He was the best oarsman in the University by some degree; a fact that he would graciously acknowledge.

He rowed for his country more than once and only missed an Olympic medal by the width of a piece of paper; the airline ticket to his summer holiday. A time and a place for everything, he said.

Despite an erratic attendance at lectures and tutorials, which he admitted to finding dull, he graduated.

Later, to enraptured female audiences he would describe his degree as 'special' which was the wording the University also used.

He had read law and to everyone's surprise, apart from the rowing community, secured a pupillage in a very grand commercial set.

There he had toiled for a year and was consequently amazed not to be offered a permanent place.

This he put down to jealousy and settled for the less

rigorous life of a general barrister. He had a chaotic flat in Chelsea, a lilac Mercedes sports car and a very full diary. He was content.

The party, when they arrived, was in full swing.

Johnny made straight for Joy while Spender dealt with his public. He then followed. Joy and he were old friends from Cambridge, secretly adored each other and disguised this by being as rude as possible.

The news of the Soldier's departure was not unexpected but welcome nonetheless and Joy's vagrant state immediately prompted offers of lodging from both men.

Joy, after some well feigned indecision, opted for Spender.

The risk of complication with Johnny was just too great and after all, Chelsea is Chelsea.

And for Johnny, that had been almost that.

He had bumped into her from time to time and heard of the inevitable divorce, but Scotland had called.

His father was ill, fatally as it turned out, and Kirkstiel had to be managed. He had not seen Joy since. But, as he turned to Joffrey, he knew that he would not be telling the entire truth.

There had been a pause, rather a long one, Johnny realised.

Joffrey was looking at his papers and blinking in an apologetic way.

What to say, and how much?

He cleared his throat and began.

Yes, of course he knew Joy, he replied and related the gist of his thoughts. Joffrey listened with studied care, occasionally making notes.

Twice he interrupted to confirm dates, although the events in question when now so long ago that Johnny himself was not entirely sure.

Thus, by this circuitous route, they reached the only real question.

Where was she now?

This, in truth, he could not answer. He knew which

country. This from the postage stamps on the Christmas card that he received every December.

However, he did not have an address, only an email account which she never seemed to check.

In any event she had made it quite clear that this information was for him alone and not to be divulged.

He knew that she did not want to be found and thought that he knew why. Money, Borders rumour had it, was missing: had been missing for some years now.

Opinion was divided as to where it had come from, and to where it had gone.

Matthew was favoured over Mrs Turnbull and if one believed Petronella, Joy had behaved as her background dictated and was nothing but a common thief.

Those who knew Petronella even slightly thought the sheer venom of her frequent denouncements suspicious.

That she complained too much.

In any case, it was hard to take seriously an emaciated and aggressive woman who drank more than was good for her, yet still had mental stamina to conjure an unkind word for any occasion.

Johnny could not believe the gossip. Joy simply was not, nor ever had been, remotely avaricious.

Yet, he had to confess, that she was, to all intents and purposes, hiding and wanted to stay hidden. The fact that a lawyer was looking for her seemed to verify this caution. He would try to probe further.

'I wonder if you would mind telling me why you're looking for Joy?' suitably neutral he thought.

The response, 'I'm afraid that I am not at liberty to divulge that information,' meant that, perhaps, the fencing had started.

Johnny realised that he must tread carefully and not inadvertently reveal more than he should.

Joffrey leaned into the attack; 'You say that she is now divorced. This, by chance, I already know. I have contacted her ex-husband who was less than helpful. He has his reasons I am sure but I find the abrupt military tone most ill mannered,' this with a thin smile.

'A poor attempt at the human touch,' thought Johnny, although he agreed with the sentiment.

'Perhaps you can tell me by what name she now goes? Has she, for example, remarried?'

This direct approach put Johnny in something of a quandary.

That she had married again he did know. Whether she was still married, divorce often becoming a habit after one has been around the course a first time, he did not. Evidently this presumed that he did not know her new surname. Her email was simply, Joy87@hotmail.com.

'Can you at least tell me whether you are looking for her on behalf another authority?'

More dangerous, thought Johnny but a position from which retreat was possible, especially if he played the upper class fool.

This time, however, a genuinely warm smile was the result.

'I have no idea what you might mean by that question, but in any event the answer is no. I need to make contact to discuss a matter germane only to me, my firm and my client. I think I am not being indiscreet by saying that, while perhaps complicated, the overall content is not unfortunate.'

This took Johnny a moment to translate, but the smile emboldened him.

'I apologise for being wary but Joy had said that if anyone came looking for her she did not want to be found. I think I know her new surname. She did remarry and, so far, there's no evidence of a subsequent divorce. I have an email address which I can't tell you, but I will mail her myself today, if you wish, and ask her to contact you, or failing that, whether I may pass on her details. I have an idea that the IT boffins can track one down electronically, so I wouldn't place too much hope on her granting me permission. Indeed, I don't think she goes to her computer much, so you may be in for a bit of a wait.'

Joffrey paused. This was something at least and he was certain that Johnny had told the truth. He had seen enough evasion and heard so many outright lies during a legal career that he could recognise honesty. In any case, he doubted Johnny's ability to dissemble.

'Thank you for being so candid', he replied, 'I would be grateful if you would do as you say.

Incidentally, we have a computer support team at my office. I will ask whether someone can be traced as you suggest. I will also enquire whether one can somehow highlight a message as urgent. However if she, as you say, does not often monitor her correspondence this may be a pointless exercise. Is there any other help at all that you are able to offer or can you suggest some other avenue that I have overlooked?'

This appeal left Johnny with a choice. He was fairly certain that Joy would not have given him alone her email address.

He could make an informed guess as to who those others might be.

The question was, what would they think if approached by an Edinburgh solicitor or, for that matter, what would Joy say if his indiscretions came to light?

He came to a decision.

He had already gone perhaps further then he should, but so far, he could see no harm. In any event, he had a man in mind.

Spender.

He must know as much as Johnny, probably more, and would certainly not be intimidated by Joffrey.

He gave the name and, from a dilapidated blue book, an address and telephone number. The only caveat he added was that, if possible, his own name not be mentioned.

This was agreed and with that the subject was closed.

They adjourned to a lunch of commiseration over Edinburgh property prices and, despite Joffrey's ignorance of the subject, the prospects for grouse that coming year.

Chapter 9

The very next morning Sir Merlin Hayley accepted the telephone call from Edinburgh.

It was mildly irritating that his habitual coffee and perusal of the pink financial press should be interrupted, but what could you expect from solicitors, especially the Scottish type?

He listened in silence, noted the salient details and acquiesced to the request.

The results, if any, he promised to relay and then he replaced the receiver.

He was not, in fact, as irked as the scowl on his face might have initially suggested. There were two reasons for this.

Firstly, he had ignored his side of the agreement for too long.

Secondly, and more importantly, the name Spender stirred his memory.

Vague impressions of a large and cocksure young man. What Sir Merlin dismissively thought of as an amateur.

This fellow had acted, he recalled, as second to an incompetent opposition in a squalid affair of fraud some years back.

The young man's lack of deference had grated and there had been no opportunity for a satisfactory put down.

He thought for a while and then lifted the telephone to start his enquiry.

The questions did not concern Joy, rather, a certain Mr Spender.

A large part of Sir Merlin's success was due to a nasty mind.

Pressure; what some might even term blackmail usually paid with results and Sir Merlin hated to leave empty-handed.

The upper echelons of the London legal scene are small and loyalties tribal and shifting. Sir Merlin, from his lofty perch in the stratosphere could perhaps be forgiven for a slightly hazy view of the legal suburbs that Spender occupied.

It was thus that he was unaware that the questions he had caused to be asked, while answered back up to him, were also reported in the opposite direction.

Spender was intrigued but puzzled to be the object of such attention.

As with all apart from saints, his immediate reaction was one of guilt.

His sins were legion and on several fronts.

A keen shooting man with an extensive and expensive armoury, he had never seen the need for permits or licences. But this was surely small beer?

Among his army of past and present girlfriends, divide and rule was his motto and none, he thought, knew of each other or were presently pregnant.

This he considered more dangerous and accordingly made a mental note.

Cars and mortgages?

Possible.

Spender's financial arrangements were byzantine in their complexity and perhaps one lender had spoken to another. If you do not open your mail how could you know? In any case, the drifts of envelopes were too deep for easy exploration.

No, Spender thought, the prime suspect must be Montmorillon.

Montmorillon or Monst, as it was known in the society pages, was a nightclub and, depending on his mood, Spenders pride and joy or sisyphean burden.

It was a private club but not of the Soho variety.

Its privacy was due largely to its location.

Tucked into the side streets of Pimlico, it was very hard to find. Many searched but sometimes the faint hearted gave up and therein lay the problem.

Turnover, or rather a lack of it. For those in the know, or who possessed a military grade GPS, it was unique and irreplaceable.

Monst had that subtle blend of retro shabby decor,

seventies music and high prices that the rich find so comforting.

Nightclubs can usually be divided into two categories; members accounts or cash only. Monst straddled this divide at the whim of its proprietor and his current financial state. Staff and liquor bills were constants, customers, sadly not.

A cash business requires the most meticulous and timely accounting, details Spender found tiresome. 'Small minded' as he had once said to Joy.

A cash business, given meticulous and timely accounting, can also be used in other roles. For example, a re-distribution of profit between companies.

As a barrister, Spender was keenly aware of this, had seen it often, even had to demonstrate to bovine juries how it was done.

In short, should he have wanted to, the reallocation of cash would have presented no problems.

It would not be quite true to say that the thought had never occurred to him but Spender was fundamentally honest.

Rightly, he hesitated further to muddy waters already murky.

In reality it was often quite impossible to say whether Monst was or was not profitable. Spender knew this and now he feared Sir Merlin Hayley also did.

Thank heaven, he thought, for offshore trust companies.

Chapter 10

The meeting came three days later.

Sir Merlin had called and Spender had feigned surprise and interest that someone so exalted would seek his counsel.

Spender's club was decided as the venue, the time early evening.

Thus, comfortably ensconced, not far from the haughty gaze of the Dilettantes, the bargaining began.

Spender, almost certain that sooner or later the evening would descend to the level of the souk, or for that matter, the courtroom, had not come unarmed.

Sir Merlin, for his part, had made the error of mistaking arrogance for stupidity. Arrogance may or may not be combined with stupidity. Pomposity, to which Sir Merlin inclined, by its very nature, almost always is.

Spender's enquiries had started with Who's Who.

He had isolated interest and pinpointed geography.

Then, using his voluminous address book, he defined and localised.

The results had been promising.

Sir Merlin had been a Conservative Member of Parliament and like all good schoolboys, Spender knew the old adage concerning power and corruption.

He had found several friends and acquaintances in Sir Merlin's old constituency. One, a large landowner, had been very helpful. Much was innuendo, more was speculation but, he thought, it should suffice.

The tabloid press dined off such fare and had far greater resources for research. For a man in search of a peerage, such interest would be fatal.

Spender was thus ready, if not actually looking forward to the contest.

The doctrine of mutually assured destruction, M A D for short, had effectively kept global peace since 1945.

It ought to work for him as well.

The conversation began with a threat. It was heavily veiled and couched in polite language but nonetheless, clear.

'Do tell me, how is the nightclub faring? It can't be easy with the city in such turmoil and all the bright young things under the American axe.'

'Odd' thought Spender; 'odd that he should start with such a bang. He must be serious.'

The reality was more straightforward. Spender was a large man, Sir Merlin was not.

He felt physically intimidated.

Despite millennia of evolution, despite centuries of education, at a subconscious level the ancient rules still held sway.

Spender realised something of the sort. He was hardly unused to the phenomenon and, in fact, it lent him confidence.

A serene calm descended on him. His shoulders relaxed, he settled deeper into his armchair and lifted his glass.

'Doing very well actually. Buggers have time on their hands and a redundancy package to spend, but thank you for your concern.'

This was untrue but stated with a lazy complacency.

Sir Merlin recognised the signals. This man would not easily be browbeaten. Perhaps it had been wrong to start as he had.

He made his second mistake.

'Incidentally, please remember me to your mother. I was very sad to see about your father. My condolences.'

This seemed to Spender equally odd.

The man was surely too experienced to retreat at the first setback? Perhaps it was a feint? Attack, withdrawal and ambush of the eager pursuit?

He had used it in court himself but this felt different. Anyway, he would not be tempted. Nor would he risk the ascendancy, be it ever so small, he seemed to have gained.

'She is well thank you; I didn't realise that you knew my parents.'

'Bastard,' thought Sir Merlin. 'He's not backing down. Far from it.'

But he had to admit that the response had been well done, an active rather than passive defence.

Surely the man had some respect for his elders and betters?

If he had known Spender longer, if he was not quite so blinded by what he took to be the splendour of his own position, Sir Merlin would not have asked himself these questions.

Rank had never overly bothered Spender, it simply did not occur to him that others might consider themselves superior.

He did know, though, that he had never heard either of his parents ever mention Sir Merlin, despite his occasional appearance on the television or in the press.

A kinder man than Spender might here have slipped the choke chain a couple of links.

Sir Merlin had dug himself a hole.

A rescuer might reasonably expect a reward.

The rescuer would have been wrong. The British legal system is adversarial. So were Spender and Sir Merlin both by nature and by nurture.

'Sink or swim,' thought Spender.

'By the time you are my age, I dare say that you also will find your children not always acquainted with everyone that you know. Forgive me, do you have children?'

This was better Spender considered.

True, the tone had lowered, become more personal.

Nonetheless, a recovery of sorts had been staged and the pretence of good fellowship revealed as the disguise it was.

Sir Merlin had shown at least part of his hand. Potentially it might be a winner.

He was gambling that Spender would not hold anything substantial and he considered it unlikely that he would or could bluff. He seemed too large and too obvious.

Not that Spender yet realised it, but Sir Merlin had just made his third mistake.

'Forgive me for being direct, but I am rather pushed for time. Please tell me how I can help you.'

And so détente established, Sir Merlin came to the subject.

He explained that he had an old established client who wished to contact a girl that he believed to be an acquaintance of Spenders.

This said with a nasty leer.

A Miss Joy Turnbull.

He did not say that his client was dead nor did he mention the concurrent Scottish search. In his view, neither detail was relevant to his query.

He knew, however, that some explanation for his assumption that Spender would have this information was needed.

This was furnished with a brief recital of his recent dinner in Cambridge. He had been reluctant to mention Westminster College knowing the views that those who had attended more ancient establishments held, but felt that, slipped in early, the name might escape comment.

In this he was mistaken as the delighted smile on Spender's face amply illustrated.

Irritated, he continued, explaining that, quite by chance, Joy's name had come up along with that of Spenders and that since other avenues had failed he felt obliged to follow this lead, however tenuous.

If this sounded weak but plausible to Sir Merlin, Spender found it positively lame.

He was sorely tempted to exploit the Westminster connection purely for his own amusement.

In his day the college had been known as Westminstero for the 'oh' that usually followed the confession of having gone there.

But this was Joy, his beloved Joy and he put away selfish indulgence.

'Who exactly was taking such liberties with my name?' He asked.

For once Sir Merlin was being truthful in answering that he did not know.

He described the large financier employed by the Americans and his coterie of companions. He described the conversation. He even mentioned what they had been drinking. Names however, eluded him.

Not so Spender.

He was fairly certain of his man and a telephone call later that evening would confirm it. Nonetheless, the fact that Joy had lodged with him could not have come from this source. The man in question had not kept up with either of them since coming down and was unlikely to have been aware of the fact.

Sir Merlin obviously had more than one source of information.

Spender decided, for the moment, to let this incongruity pass. Joy's wishes were quite clear. She wanted to remain private.

Spender had an idea for the reason behind this and had no intention of admitting anything.

He agreed that some twenty three or twenty four years ago she had taken a room with him for a few months.

In fact it had been for over a year. Since then contact had been more sporadic. He might be able to find out more, he said, but why?

What was this client's interest?

This Sir Merlin would not divulge, nor his client's name. It was partly professional etiquette and partly a growing dislike for this obscure girl whom everyone seemed to adore.

There was also a keening of interest in Spender, or so it seemed to him, that suggested he was not being entirely open.

It was not enough to offer to 'ask around' as Spender had said he would; Sir Merlin needed names and places. Perhaps a further allusion to the nightclub would provide the necessary stimulus.

It was his fourth and last mistake of the evening.

'Well thank you for your time and the drink. I will not hold you back further. I'm sure that the management of a nightclub, despite the glamour, needs a steady pair of hands. Please let me know if anything comes to mind.'

Spender tilted his head and took the proffered hand. He played his trump.

'Thank you Sir Merlin. Actually I'm having dinner with

Archie Lloyd this evening. Now I come to think of it, wasn't he one of your former constituents? I'm lucky enough to shoot with him most years. Such wonderful country and a beautiful estate with all its woods and little cottages. You must know him?'

Sir Merlin did, indeed, know Archie Lloyd.

He knew even better the cottage that he rented from the estate in an assumed name.

It was his secret retreat and the friends he entertained there, he wished also to keep secret.

Spender, he belatedly realised, had called him.

The wretched man had bluffed and the hands were equal.

No more nightclubs, at least for the moment..

They shook hands and went their separate ways.

The upshot of these two meetings, Johnny with Joffrey and the more prickly encounter between Spender and Sir Merlin were two emails sent to Joy's address.

They did not receive the prompt and full attention that they merited.

Chapter 11

Petronella was impatient.

Her life seemed to her to have been made up entirely of waiting, a dreary antechamber composed of last year's magazines with a stagnant fish tank for company.

Certainly the other attendees moved on but not, it seemed, she.

In another person this might have produced some degree of stoicism or at least a resigned fatalism.

Not so Petronella.

The delay merely stoked a simmering and bitter resentment.

Life, she considered, had been hard on her and if she seemed petulant to her dwindling band of friends, that impression was lost on her.

Why, she continually asked herself, the hold-up? Her father, Matthew, was long gone and Andrea had finally seen fit to do the decent thing and also quit the scene.

Why couldn't that common little man Joffrey release her long overdue and rightful inheritance?

She had been aghast and very angry all those years ago to learn that Matthew had left his estate in Andrea's favour.

From the moment that he was pronounced dead she had started, mentally for the most part, to spend his money, only to realise that the sentimental fool had thwarted her ambition with dreary legal clauses and trustees to watch over them.

At least she considered, Andrea had been prevented from blowing the lot, which would have certainly been its fate otherwise. However, it was she who should have held the purse strings, not some wretched crew of grey Edinburgh professionals.

For those who knew her this was a constant theme. An endlessly repeated gripe.

Among the more perceptive, a growing minority, this was the essence of Petronella.

An embittered individual since childhood with a schizophrenic contradiction at heart. For Petronella was, at the same time, a spendthrift wastrel but yet a miserly Scrooge, jealously brooding over her hoarded loot.

She did not love living things, or so it seemed to the outside world, only the dusty objects that crowded her dirty house and overflowed into her ramshackle outbuildings.

She had certainly never shown affection to her parents. Only a parody of that emotion when she wanted something. Her four children had been pawns, often sacrificed **in** the constant power struggle with Andrea. They, wisely, had removed themselves from her grasp as soon as they were old enough.

Elsa only registered as someone who would dilute the eventual pot and Joy, if thought of at all, had been a wasteful and ridiculous indulgence on her father's part.

Her childhood had been a litany of school expulsions and disappointed boyfriends. She did not do girlfriends. There seemed no point.

In other children this might have resulted in shyness or a lack of self confidence. Petronella was made of sterner stuff.

Doubt and unhappiness in others represent opportunity to the unscrupulous: Petronella used a long and thorough apprenticeship to good effect.

She had not been without talent at the start.

She could ride well, was fearless out hunting.

When it suited her, she could be amusing; good occasional company, assuming that the drink was flowing and a victim to hand.

Those weaker than her she cultivated. Those stronger were derided with salacious gossip behind their backs.

She had been, briefly, pretty but an insatiable appetite for late nights and alcohol had started the process of erosion and the result, whilst still a work in progress, was anything but.

Surprisingly she had married. All had agreed that Malcolm was a decent man, perhaps rather work shy but luckily possessed of that inestimable quality; a large portfolio of blue chip securities.

The honeymoon had, in one sense, never started and in another, never ended.

Despite Malcolm being Dutch a house had been purchased close to Gladdies so that Petronella might keep her beady eye on affairs.

The party had continued.

The alcoholic fringe of Glasgow society descended, often for weeks at a time. Despite the lack of sobriety, children were conceived, born and neglected.

Money was spent without reckoning and a general air of seediness spread itself, like a tablecloth, over the young couple.

Malcolm's old friends and family despaired. He seemed bewitched. Paralysed and unable to extract himself from the morass into which he was sinking.

If Petronella noticed, she didn't care.

The daily round of pointless drinking with hopeless people continued and quietly, privately, Malcolm descended into a deep depression. As seemed inevitable, tragedy was the outcome. A car. In his case an oak tree and exhaustion on return from his beloved and bewildered sister in Maastricht.

Matthew was not alone in later pondering the possible link between mental state and physical effect.

As was her want, Petronella flourished. She rapidly transformed herself into a latter day Queen Victoria, albeit with a bottle instead of sceptre.

This was what Joy remembered.

She was not, however surprised.

Petronella had very little of Matthew in her makeup.

Nor was Andrea the culprit. The original had kept, at first, in the shadows; initially proud but latterly, increasingly, in fear of her double. Andrea's mother, Maud was the architect with countless instances of carefully engineered favouritism.

This wicked brew had stewed and bubbled for some fifty years and the resulting vintage was a subtle mix of low cunning and high paranoia.

Petronella saw conspiracy everywhere.

Her parents were gone, there was a will, she was the eldest, thus everything must be hers. The tedious legal process of probate held no meaning for her.

Delay was suspicious, an alliance of lawyers, trustees and family conspiring to cheat her. She had acted.

The abrupt request to view the Will had come as no surprise to Joffrey.

He knew Petronella and her ways of old and recalled, with a shudder, the scene after Matthew's death.

This new demand had the same hallmarks.

Another 'friend' with, apparently, legal background would accompany her to decipher, indeed read, the text.

There was no need for any trustee to attend; all she wanted was privacy.

This last, at least, he could ensure and Joffrey made a careful note in his diary to be absent from his office on the day in question.

One of his unfortunate subordinates could receive this particular broadside. A useful if, he suspected, extreme lesson in client relationships.

Petronella had duly arrived in shabby splendour, trailing a small nervous man who the office later reported smelled strongly of drink.

Or perhaps it was them both.

In any event they had remained ensconced alone for some fifty minutes talking in muffled tones with occasional loud and rude punctuation.

They had emerged, Joffrey was told by his junior in awed tones, like a sudden thunderclap.

Made strident and public accusations of fraud, a promise to sue and then left to the slamming of doors, the 'friend' looking even more dishevelled and miserable than before. It was much as he had anticipated and he knew that he could now look forward to a succession of long, rambling and barely literate letters. All rude and all recorded delivery. He sighed.

Where on earth was Joy? He must find her or run the certain risk of more Petronella. It was a powerful incentive.

Chapter 12

Uncouth as her methods were, Petronella's suspicions were not entirely unjustified.

Joffrey too had questions which he could not answer although, in his experience, chaos was more likely the culprit than conspiracy.

Nonetheless, there were, he admitted, gaps in the narrative.

Voids where there should have been text and holes where before there were objects. Matthew, as he had reason to recall, had owned many virtues but bookkeeping was not among them.

An old, war time, friend of dubious ability had helped him with his accounts.

Joffrey had made enquiries but the friend was dead and any records kept, long since discarded.

There were sealed letters, only to be opened at the final division of Matthew's legacy. A promise of final closure yet at present a hindrance.

Petronella might not sue as she had threatened, but as Joffrey knew all too well, Scotland is a little pond and mud tends to stick.

There was also an inventory compiled not long before Matthew's death. It was between this inventory, the accounts and his will that the problem, his problem, lay.

Specifically, there were three problems.

Firstly, cash. Some £100,000.

Secondly, bearer share certificates in a turn of the century Canadian mining company. Once worthless, now not.

Finally, a large and splendid portrait of Matthew's maternal grandfather, magnificent in court regalia and bearing the small but significant signature: Reynolds.

In all, and depending on the market, a considerable sum was missing and there was no obvious destination or exact time of departure.

They had been in the inventory. The cash featured in the last set of accounts. The picture in an early draft of the will, they were not there now.

The problem, as Joffrey well knew, was not a lack of suspects but the opposite.

Both Andrea and Petronella had motive and opportunity.

Andrea's mother was certainly capable and Elsa and Joy, although less likely, could not be discounted.

It was clear that Petronella had her own ideas.

As ever with her, these were not opinions, although much broadcast, widely shared.

She discounted her mother as too stupid.

In any event, Petronella had kept a sleepless watch over the contents of Gladdies since Matthew's death, rightly suspecting that Andrea would attempt some covert sales to fund her grandmother's lifestyle.

This reign had begun gently, camouflaged as daughterly concern for a grieving widow.

It had soon become absolute, imposed ruthlessly and had slowly, but surely, driven all but the hardiest visitors away.

Andrea had become, as was Petronella's aim, a prisoner in her own house, afraid to take any decision unless first suggested and approved by her daughter.

Some trinkets had indeed gone the grandmother's way, but these had been significant only in as much as they cemented the old alliance of control over Andrea.

She had not been able to exert the same power over Elsa.

Her younger sister had married well and moved south.

Visits, infrequent since Matthew's death, had latterly ceased altogether.

Petronella was behind this; repelling Elsa while taking every opportunity to denounce her sister's absence as uncaring and spoiled.

Revelling in her sole dominion, Petronella knew that Andrea would not have dared slip presents into Elsa's hands for she had poisoned her mind against her younger sister.

This left Joy.

Joy, the housekeeper's daughter; a girl with no prospects

of her own but an appetite whetted by the environment she had charitably been allowed to share.

Matthew, the weak fool, had always kept a part of his heart for her.

Had insisted that they were raised as equals; given the same rights and affection.

Joy had shamelessly traded on this trust, always sweet, willing and unassuming. No tantrums, merely a desire to please; and why wouldn't she, given the alternative?

An obvious sham to cover clutching greed.

Petronella did not consider love. She had, obviously, heard of it, but in her experience it was an ephemeral emotion quickly superseded by the real politic of power and clawing addiction of cash.

Love was too delicate to last, too easily broken by the urge for more and the lust for new sensation.

She judged, as most do, by her own standards, thereby mistaking the obvious and replacing it with a calculating, avaricious manipulation.

Given the level of public indiscretion to which Petronella was want, it was not surprising that her immediate circle and then, by gossipy percolation, the more general Dumfriesshire society became aware of skulduggery at Gladdies.

The very fact of Petronella, while often deplored, was, by virtue of her tiny size and enormous volume, hard to ignore.

Sadly, for her, public opinion drew its own conclusion.

There is a crescendo at which denunciation turns in on itself and becomes self defeating. Most assumed that a smokescreen was being laid by the real perpetrator and that the root of the problem was Petronella.

Her magpie tendencies were well-known, along with her single- minded determination to have her own way.

Certainly this was Joffrey's opinion.

For him, Petronella had protested too much and prosecuted Joy with unusual vigour.

The money was hard to understand but enfeebled men have been known to do strange things as death approaches and resolve drains away.

He could well imagine a domineering Petronella browbeating her father until a cheque or bankers draft was wrung out of him.

The evidence of several large withdrawals was there, the destination not.

Bearer share certificates were more problematical.

As their name implies, he who physically holds them owns them.

There was no record of title in register, nor transaction history.

The old fashioned safe in Matthew's office had been their repository since his mother's death.

They were not there now and he felt certain that Petronella, perhaps alone, knew the combination to the safe.

The picture. It was vast, even by Victorian standards. Would have needed at least two men and a van to move it and considerable space to house it.

For his money, it would be found in the Aladdin's cave that was Petronella's home. That, at least, he consoled himself, should be reasonably easy to resolve.

Finally the sealed letters, only to be opened at the end. He knew their contents for he had helped draft them.

Their very presence was a frantic irritation to Petronella and the subject of wild speculation.

He could not even begin to imagine her reaction to what was revealed.

It was a moment he looked forward to with an equal mixture of dread and anticipation. But first he must find Joy, and that as soon as possible. Before Petronella's storm of accusation began to gain credibility through the very weight of monotonous repetition.

Chapter 13

If Joffrey had troubles with client proximity, the same could not be said for Sir Merlin Hayley.

For lawyers, clients are an unfortunate part of the revenue earning process, and Sir Merlin found their silly questions and mundane worries just as tiresome as did Joffrey. However, he had taken care to avoid too much personal contact unless, of course, they had that combination of breeding and wealth he found so alluring.

Better, he considered, to keep them at arm's length with a buffer zone of solicitors and accountants.

Familiarity breeds contempt. Sir Merlin rarely risked the former.

It was thus he found himself contemplating the sun setting into the Atlantic Ocean through the stem of a glass of exquisitely dry sherry. He was on his quarterly visit to the Channel Island of Jersey, an odd place that attracted people who could easily afford better.

He was here on Playfair Trust business. A business so dear to his heart and future comfort that he deigned to make the trip in person. For him, as for many others, Jersey had special virtues.

It was true, he conceded, that his hotel was comfortingly expensive and the view over the southern sweep of St Ouen's Bay magnificently wild, but the island had changed since he first started coming here in the late 1960s and not, in his opinion, for the better.

The Jersey that he remembered when he first came had been gentler and much more agricultural. There had been, of course, a burgeoning financial sector blessed by a tax regime that shone brightly through the murk of England's socialist experiment. It was the reason that bought him here. But the rich had been fewer and ostentation was not yet in vogue.

For the most part, pretty granite farmhouses still had mud,

cows and tractors. They had not yet sprouted vast hedges of Leylandia guarding acres of security lit tarmac.

The accents that one heard were either that of the Madeiran labour force or that curious burr of ancient Norman French that sounds, to the untutored ear, slightly South African. The roads were lanes, deep, private and meandering, reflecting their Norman bocage heritage and a traffic jam meant the twice daily trek to the milking parlour, not some blonde botulox unable to reverse her Ferrari.

This scene of bucolic calm had accommodated the annual summer influx of holidaymakers, the third tier of the islands economy. It was a more innocent age, as yet uncorrupted by cheap flights and the lure of the exotic. The British had still preferred only a modicum of foreigness and Jersey, so close to the French coast, but only half abroad, was a good compromise.

The hotel where Sir Merlin sat comfortably could not have existed then. Accommodation had been a choice of endless 'Sea View' guest houses, Butlins or hotels sinking genteelly into senility.

Jersey had become becalmed in the 1950s and for a certain type of British tourist this was deeply reassuring.

The island had slumbered on through the 1970s like a pensioner in a suburban retirement home. It was not that the islanders were unaware of changes in the world around them, but they seemed unable to grasp and direct their own future.

Agriculture had moved on, both North to the low countries and South to Spain. The Common Market meant new potatoes, daffodils and winter cauliflower were no longer Jersey's exclusive fiefdom. Economies of scale and the abolition of import tariffs had put paid to that. The British customer, in theory, preferred the Jersey label but he was fickle and his hand increasingly did not follow his heart.

So too tourism. The Jersey climate cannot compete with Iberian sun. Television had opened his eyes and Freddie Laker his wallet. Britain flew south, leaving the island to those in search of nostalgia. Sadly, it is casinos and bars that take the easy money. Museums and mementos of the German occupation are a harder sell and one by one the guest houses wilted.

It was not all decay. As traditional Jersey died a new community was born on the back of the fabulous wealth generated by London in the 1980s. These rich were different to their parents. They ventured farther and farther afield to holiday. They ate whatever they wanted regardless of season. It is always Spring somewhere in the world.

Most importantly, they understood money. How it is made, how it is lost, and they had an especial horror of giving it to the tax man.

There are many fiscal havens in the world and they often offer better rates than Jersey. What they do not always have is the stability and respectability that centuries of British underpinning endow.

Many, in fact, are little better than the Wild West, more or less concealed under a thin legal veneer.

The large financial institutions, be they brokers, bankers, accountants or trust companies were quick to recognise this. They came in their droves and the money, vast amounts, followed.

Jersey was back on the map and the early morning red eye flight from London increasingly packed with Sir Merlin and his like.

They catered for a wide variety of clients but, generally speaking, these could be placed into two main categories; before and after the goldrush.

Sir Merlin, he was pleased to think, catered mainly for the former.

These were the older British establishment of inherited wealth.

Those who had been born with their money and had neither the wit nor inclination to continue increasing the pot.

They had what they had and contented themselves with living off the interest, something easier to do if one does not share a significant proportion with the Inland Revenue.

They had been arriving in the island as a steady trickle since the 1950s, picked the best houses and considered the new wave as little better than parvenus.

They were the aristocracy of tax avoiders and doyen amongst them had been Alice Playfair.

Jersey had claimed her in the mid-1960s, held her captive for over thirty five years and finally released her some months past.

She had come passively at Sir Merlin's prompting. She had not been hard to persuade as, at that time, she felt her life to be already over.

The broken engagement with Matthew, her only true love. The brutal separation from her baby girl whose whereabouts no amount of pleading would reveal.

It had been for her own health they said, the child was in a happy and caring family and no good would come of complicating the situation.

The sad and lonely sojourn in Switzerland and subsequent short lived marriage to an older man she hardly knew.

He had been her father's choice and had quickly revealed himself as a feckless drunk and bully. The divorce that she demanded had been quickly agreed after production of horrifying evidence of abuse.

The shock had been too much for her parents.

Her father, apoplectic with rage at her presumption, had suffered a massive stroke. Her mother, subservient to the last, had meekly followed in his footsteps some few months later, leaving Alice alone in the world.

Her first thoughts had been to fly to Matthew but he was married and she could not bear to break his heart again.

So to Jersey it was; where she sank gratefully into anonymous torpor cocooned by the insular island culture.

While one breathes, life goes on and the healing power of dogs, she thought, should never be underestimated. Sir Merlin had acquired, on her behalf, a house and garden in the parish of St John.

It was a large building of the type known to the islanders as a Cod house.

There were several of these dotted around Jersey, built by suddenly rich trawler owners on the back of the Newfoundland Great Banks cod bonanza of the 1800s.

The garden, about five acres, was an overgrown muddle

and her only neighbours the small placid brown cows for which Jersey is also famous.

In short, Sir Merlin could hardly have picked a less suitable place for a damaged and lonely young woman; which may well have been his aim all along.

There were no heirs and he was her guardian and sole trustee.

Epiphany, when it came, was small, cowed and black.

Alice had been vaguely aware during those first grey months of an occasional nocturnal visitor.

The most tangible evidence was a ransacked dustbin.

Jersey does not have foxes.

Once, she had caught a daylight glimpse but, aware that it was being watched, it had fled. Intrigued, despite her general despondence, she had left milk and the remains of her supper outside the kitchen and waited.

In the main she fed hedgehogs but from time to time was rewarded by a timid black visitor. This became a habit, almost a high point in her day and little by little, food bred a wary trust.

One evening the dog did not come.

This was a surprise and, she realised, a disappointment.

On a whim she went out, although she hardly expected to see anything as the night was moonless and dark.

What she could not see, she heard and to her the sound was as vivid as a flashlit photograph.

It was a dog whimpering in pain.

She rushed inside and despite her fluster found a torch.

Underneath an ancient rhododendron at the left of back courtyard was a small black dog lying on its side.

It was bloated, with a muzzle flecked with spittle, indeed, in the torch beam the only sign of life were a pair of ebony eyes, wide with terror.

She did not hesitate. After all the hurt and loss, here was someone worse off and finally she could be master of her own destiny. Gently she scooped the unresisting body into her arms, returned and laid it on the carpet in front of the fire.

Veterinary surgeons are probably as close to saints as the modern world comes, and the long suffering locum at the St Lawrence Practice took the slightly hysterical call from a strange woman in her stride.

Yes, despite the hour, she would go to the surgery; a rendezvous in say, half an hour?

To her surprise the caller was waiting when she got there.

The rich, and by her accent the caller certainly was, often think nothing of making those less well off wait.

The dog had been poisoned, by what and how it was impossible to say. What was certain was that Alice had saved a life, she did not need veterinary opinion to confirm this.

Days turned into a week but finally the drip was unhooked, the catheter removed and the dog could go.

He had no microchip, no tattoo; there were no anxious announcements concerning a lost friend in the local evening paper.

He was effectively an orphan, as alone and vulnerable as his saviour. She sensed this, he knew it

. Home would be, in the physical sense, a Cod house. But home is also where you are cherished and thus it proved.

She named him Mungo after the patron saint of Glasgow, for he had something of the Gorbals about him.

He was a dog for all seasons, by day intrepid hunter, at night, hot water bottle.

Breeding, or what he had, was uncertain, tending to terrier.

Beyond all doubt however, was his effect on Alice. It is impossible to rest sad and neutral in the face of canine enthusiasm.

Dogs and cigarettes breed acquaintance. Acquaintances become friends. So it proved.

To Sir Merlin's alarm Alice had cast off from the shore of despondency never to return.

He had never much liked dogs.

He now liked them even less.

With her life rekindled, earlier passions resurfaced. The horse.

Jersey possesses several magnificent beaches where at

low tide one can gallop one's fill. There is also a hunt, albeit drag, but hunters are hunters and their world is small, peopled by those who know and worship the same Gods.

Alice was at home, her boat had reached harbour and she entered Jersey society.

Sadly, for Sir Merlin and his long term plans, none of this came cheap.

True, she had money enough and some to spare, but racehorse trainers, both English and French, have a voracious burn rate and the Newmarket sales are not for the faint-hearted.

Despite his warnings and entreaties, over the years, Alice spent.

There was only one account sacrosanct, that endowed for her lost child.

She realised that this was probably a forlorn hope but her intuition told her that Sir Merlin knew more than he would admit.

In any case, she had never subscribed to the view that money is more a curse than a blessing.

She held it a fiction touted by the haves to console those less lucky.

At the time of her death Alice was still a rich lady. Horses apart, her main passion had become the search for her lost daughter. Sir Merlin had not, indeed would not, help so she had turned elsewhere.

There was a man she had met, ex-military now retired to Jersey for the usual reasons. He could, apparently, 'find' things.

To her untutored eye he seemed staid enough and typical of his species.

Tweedy, slightly chinless and seemingly concerned only with sailing and golf.

It was rumoured that his past had not been so innocent and cocktail gossip had it that, from time to time, he still kept his hand in.

As was her way, Alice approached the subject directly. A telephone call, an afternoon chat at the Cod house and the question was posed. Could he help?

The man was not unduly surprised.

He had been privy to many secrets during his career and was aware of what was whispered about his past.

Moreover, had a soft spot for the old lady; he would take bluntness over flannel every time. He did not promise but agreed to talk to a man he knew in London. A response could he expected, yes or no, within the week.

What ever he had said worked .A meeting was arranged for Alice in London. Sir Merlin was not consulted.

Chapter 14

He was not what she had expected and in a strange way this gave her hope.

The private detective, as he styled himself, had stipulated the place, a bar, and a time. He was late.

Just as she was making ready to leave, he, with anything but quiet discretion, arrived. His mode of transport was a large motorbike and he was dressed to suit.

He knew, obviously, what he was looking for as he made straight for her table, shook her hand and offered profuse apologies.

His greeting was a surprise, he may have looked the biker but the accent spoke of gentler antecedents.

She was later to learn that he had many voices to match many situations. The one constant was his attire. Grubby.

That he was intelligent was immediately obvious. He knew her Jersey friend of old, had been well briefed and looked upon the task as repaying old favours.

Only he knew how many and in what currency, but there were many and he had been assured that a resolution of this old lady's problem would go some way to wiping the slate clean.

He would accept expenses, would not take a fee and would try his best. Again, no promises.

This was all explained slowly and clearly, interspersed with brusque interjections aimed at the bar staff. He seemed to know them extraordinarily well; so well in fact, that he helped himself to frequent refills without comment on their part. She could not help but ask.

'Oh that. Don't worry, je suis le patron. Cover, we used to call it in the old days.'

A naughty twinkle in the eyes, swish of the ponytail and twitch of moustache as he raised his glass to her.

His nickname was Ganesh he said. He did have a real name but no one used it, not even his wife.

He had a contact in the National Records Office who would do what he called 'a little rifling' and they would take it from there.

Yes, he understood the need for discretion concerning Sir Merlin. Did not however, foresee a problem.

He and Sir Merlin moved in very different ponds he said.

His was deeper and much less brightly lit. He doubted 'very sincerely' that, even if curious, the lawyer would risk a dip.

Alice had returned home heartened. Even the illusion of progress, if that was what it was, she found comforting. She merely wished that she had started her search earlier.

Despite appearances, Ganesh was a quick worker and confidential adoption records were well within his nefarious scope.

He had however drawn a blank and this irritated him. He telephoned- in with the result and further questions.

It was times and places that he needed and once ascertained, the cause of his perplexity became clear.

In his past life assumptions had been dangerous, sometimes lethal. Alice was self evidently British, resident in Jersey since her early thirties. He had therefore assumed certain facts.

Why she had not mentioned Switzerland he could not say, but it meant that he had been rummaging in the wrong place. His expertise did not extend to the Swiss.

They are a very private nation and take good care to keep it that way. However, he knew a certain gentleman, a Swiss national, who had some experience in running down information of this sort.

He thought it the type of problem that would intrigue him. Accordingly, she should expect a call from a Mr Richard Ribbonage.

'I'm sure you'll like him. He's an old fashioned deb's delight, concealing the alarming brain of a physics don. He'll let me know how he gets on and if the trail leads back to England, I'll take it from there.'

A call did not come. A letter arrived in its stead.

It bore a Zurich postmark and was written in a neat formal English, slightly antiquated and foreign, as if the author had stepped out of a John Buchan novel.

Mr Ribbonage apologised for not using the telephone but he had no faith in long distance calls.

He happened to be resting, between what he did not say, but as lucky chance would have it, he was visiting relations in Dinard the next week and could take the ferry over if it was convenient?

Perhaps she could let him know by return as he was not long in leaving.

She replied that day in the affirmative and out of curiosity rang Ganesh to confirm the odd letter.

'Quirky. That's Big Rick all right, very quirky. It sounds as if he's got phone trouble. Nosy sods the Swiss. Don't worry, as I said, you'll like him but be sure you've got the drinks tray well stocked. Bonne chance, madame. I'll be in touch.'

Alice settled, as so often, to wait. The furtive world, she decided, was intriguing. Certainly more stimulating than ladies bridge at the Royal Yacht Club.

Chapter 15

Unlike Ganesh, Mr Ribbonage was on time.

Exactly on time.

She watched with incredulity as a small red hire car rolled up her short drive. It seemed to be entirely filled with human being.

He emerged laughing and talking immediately, eyes smiling and outstretched hand proffered.

She could see at once that he was shy and had that gentleness the way that only truly big men have. A body language that withholds yet reassures as if to say, 'Don't be afraid, I can't help being this size'.

'Eighteen hands if he's an inch' she thought.

Crinkly black hair cut short; curly black beard ditto.

Not thin, like some very tall men, but not fat either.

To see Ribbonage at a distance was to see an ordinary man. It was only when one drew near that one realised one's error.

He was closer than you thought and scaled up to twice life-size.

She had offered to collect him from the harbour. He had declined the lift but accepted a bed for the night. It was early evening, time for a drink; Alice knew already that Ganesh was right.

She was going to like Mr.Ribbonage.

He had viewed his room and approved.

His luggage, and there was a considerable amount, was taken from car to hall and certain of it back again; they could now relax.

Alice had been silently amused by the process. It had been deliberate and rather ponderous, reminding her of going through the customs barrier at the German border when she was a child. Everything had been examined, noted and commented on; not all was exactly to his liking.

The bath, for example, was good, although the taps in the

middle were awkward. The shower, for some private reason, not.

In any event, they were now seated after careful chair selection in the smaller of her drawing rooms, she with a gin and he a very dark whiskey.

There had been method in the pedantry of Ribbonage's approach.

As a giant he was well used to being stared at.

His strategy was, metaphorically, to stare back.

This he did with meticulous attention to small detail. It had the effect of turning curiosity back on itself, the gawpers and their sidekicks becoming the centre of attention and comment, rather than he.

As camouflage, it was effective and usually bought him time to merge into the background.

It also gave him space to assess whatever confronted him and to choose his approach. The fussy, old-maidish, start was merely the precursor to an incisive and direct train of thought and action; for Ribbonage's intellect equalled his body.

He was very, very clever.

They had started with small talk and sensing a friendly manner behind initial awkwardness, Ribbonage spoke of himself. Confession, he found, lowered an opponent's guard, put the shy client at ease and went a long way to opening future doors.

He was, he said a 'batard'. A melange of two distinct races, in his case, Canadian and Swiss, although, as he noted, the Swiss were already a complicated mix.

Better, perhaps, to use the noun 'Tyrol'.

As a result he was competent in several European languages.

English in which he spoke, French for the written word and German for dreams. He had studied at the universities of Berne, Cologne and, briefly, Oxford.

When national service came around he had been too large for a tank, too refined for the infantry and had thus found himself posted to intelligence.

Unlike more conventional armies he explained, Swiss military intelligence was exactly that, not oxymoronic.

He had made some useful friends and many vile acquaintances.

Ganesh he numbered among the former. The latter peopled the novels he said were his main occupation although not yet, sadly, published.

He had experience tracing people, mainly anarchists or Irish, through Switzerland's labyrinthine bureaucracy with all its cutouts and cul-de-sacs and understood from Ganesh that something of this sort was required.

Could she, please, enlighten him further?

So Alice retold her story to the present. He was a good listener, his only utterances to confirm or query facts. He took no notes, concentrating on his glass and later, at table, his plate. He was a fastidious eater Alice soon realised, pushing food around, careful to match texture and flavour to some private recipe. He did not seem to eat enough to sustain such a large frame and she wondered whether one of his several suitcases contained a Swiss midnight feast.

He retired to bed after two large digestifs, Mirabelle was one of his favourites he said. He had given an upbeat assessment of her problem. It was solvable and probably quite quickly. He would reflect during the night and make his proposal at breakfast. This would detail likely timings and, with a sad smile, the amount needed for bribes.

He found it a terrible tragic story and was enchanted by it. Accordingly he would not charge, merely recoup expenses. It would be a pleasure to reunite mother and daughter.

The gleam in his eye said it all.

Alice, she thought, was likely to feature in some future manuscript.

It would be written in French, peopled with Anglophone characters, Teutonic in its profundity and utterly unpublishable.

In short, her privacy was assured.

Chapter 16

The answer to her question took longer to arrive than Alice had been led to expect. It was also frustratingly incomplete.

There was a name, address and even a telephone number. Alice had rung this immediately, only to hear the sad beeping of no connection.

Further calls quickly established that the address and number pertained to a discrete but long since closed Glasgow nursing home. It had dealt, apparently, with recuperating alcoholics.

The name had been, perhaps, one of the medical staff. Nurse, sister or even matron.

The baby had been styled as care of this Miss. Furndass, which had seemed odd even to Ribbonage. It was, he ventured, perhaps more of a forwarding address than final destination.

To Ganesh he had used the more professional description of 'Cut out'.

In any event, Miss. Furndass had gone, presumably with the baby, and had left no forwarding address or any other means of contact.

Alice was a step further along the road but beginning to realise that miracles are for the Bible. Those less blessed had to draw on reserves of patience and the less than divine skills of men such as Ganesh.

The letter, when it came, was not unexpected but annoying nonetheless. Ganesh had not forgotten his promise to Alice Playfair.

He did not have a brain given to amnesia, in his earlier life that would have been suicide. Rather, Ganesh had hoped that Big Rick would have solved the mystery with his customary panache, although he knew that the time scale involved meant any address might be out of date.

Nonetheless, there was a name and a British address. This

91

meant his, rather than Swiss, elbow grease. Still it would make a change from his bar.

He had been grumpy of late. Football matches and their associated supporters. He loathed both. British weather, high staff turnover, with lovesick Latvians and Slovaks taking four finger discounts from the till.

No, a change would do him good.

He turned a professional eye to the letter from Alice. That name, 'Furndass': not one he had ever come across before and he had heard many during sixteen years in the army. Perhaps it was foreign?

He brooded a little and then, in what he would later claim as a stroke of inspiration but was really boredom, decided to ring Big Rick.

He was not there.

A mobile number proved luckier although the line was charged with static. Rick, it transpired, was in Mali on, he claimed, his honeymoon.

Ganesh had not known of a girlfriend let alone a marriage and his voice betrayed his amazement.

Rick explained. It was all perfectly clear. He had met an Austrian Swede in Cambodia. They had been married in a civil ceremony on Stuart Island, New Zealand. They were now on honeymoon in Mali and would return in three months for a formal wedding in Switzerland before going to Uganda for his research. Obviously, Ganesh would be invited to the nuptials. And, by the way, what did he know about the semi nomadic Hausa and Fulani tribes?

Ganesh knew from experience of Big Rick's ability to talk and his catholic range of interests but could only imagine what mobile airtime to Mali cost. He started to ask his question but Rick was there before him.

'I knew that the Playfair file would bounce back to you and I am aware of your scepticism concerning foreigners. I've sent you photocopies of what I found; you will find everything you need. I must go, tea time. Kiss your wife's hand for me.' And he was gone.

It took a couple of minutes to process the chaos of Big Rick's reply. Ganesh knew he had been treated to the reverse of the technique used on Alice. Instead of measured pedantry he had been rushed with random facts. It was merely, he realised, Big Rick's way of saying,

'I'm on my honeymoon. For heaven's sake, go away and leave me alone.'

Sadly, he had to call again the next day. Rick did not answer. It had taken a long and irritating hour to find the letter from Big Rick.

If not as chaotic as the filing system used by Spender, postal reception and subsequent action chez Ganesh was often a hit and miss affair.

His wife toiled long hours in a subterranean office, organised everything and smoothed frequently ruffled feathers.

Ganesh did not work back office, he was strictly front of house, client interface and all that that involved.

To his many friends this job description could be summed up more succinctly with the single word 'drinking'.

When found, the letter had been erroneously filed under 'wine suppliers: Europe.' Given the Swiss stamp on the envelope it was, he supposed, a more logical choice than might have been the case.

The contents were sparse. Two sheets of paper. A compliments slip from Rick and a photo- copy of the Swiss adoption certificate.

He noted that it was not embossed with a Cantonal or National seal. Evidently this had been a very private and exclusive arrangement; something not unknown in that country. The certificate itself looked expensive.

It was a handwritten document in indecipherable Gothic calligraphy, a script much loved by the German mentality.

Ganesh assumed the language was German but even that was not certain. Only the Glasgow address was clear, but that had already been tried.

Feeling slightly guilty and more than a little foolish he had engaged the translating power of first, his wife and then the antique and rare book seller in the shop across the road. Both had pronounced it German but been defeated by the calligraphy.

93

He rang Alice, getting her at the second attempt. She merely confirmed what he already suspected; that Big Rick had included a fair copy translation with her letter. Hence her ability to read the rune-like figures.

Nonetheless, Ganesh was not convinced.

However much he squinted and turned the paper, he could not see the word 'Furndass.' At one stage of his career he had been in the Scots Guards and, to him, this name had no place in 1960s Scotland.

Thus it was that the next morning found him at the Victoria and Albert Museum where he knew someone.

The man in question had at one time worked for Ganesh's old employers. His particular skill was documents from further east, but he too had contacts and the request was laughably simple; straightforward translation. He should have a result in a couple of days.

It did not take that long.

A colleague had seen the certificate lying on his desk as he idly puzzled over it and immediately asked what such a vulgar and phoney piece of paper was doing in their august museum.

It was, she had said, typical of the many types of certificate printed in Switzerland at the end of the last war.

They were deliberately hard to decipher as a thin veneer of protection for the fraudsters and confidence tricksters who peddled them.

There was a standard format of meaningless legal gobbledygook overlaid with the relevant information desired by the client.

This, by the looks of it, was an adoption certificate from a very discreet and expensive private clinic.

She doubted if the written names had ever had any basis in reality and in any event, 'Turnbull' was pretty common in Scotland was it not?

Armed with a name in which he had more confidence Ganesh put his particular skill set in motion. His first action was to text Big Rick. It was not, by his standards, a rude message, merely a desire to confirm the new name, albeit couched in language of fake humility.

No one likes to be proved wrong and Big Rick least of all.

A response came quickly.

It did not confess error, merely pointed out that, as with all translation, the meaning given to any word was at the whim and nuance of the expert.

For Ganesh, the difference between 'Furndass' and 'Turnbull' amounted to more than creative interpretation and, in this case, he preferred English expertise over Swiss.

Big Rick must truly be in love, he thought, to have taken his eye so completely off the ball.

His second action was cyber research.

The Internet revealed almost twenty Scottish medical associations, complete with current contact details. It seemed probable that at least one amongst them could shed light on the defunct Glasgow establishment and thereby erstwhile members of staff; someone who might recall a Miss. Turnbull.

His third, and for the moment final, action was to ring Alice.

Sadly. No.

Although the name tweaked some memory, that was not entirely unexpected. She knew of at least two Trainers called Turnbull and several greyhounds, if that helped.

She would call back if something else came to mind but certainly he could offer a reward for information.

The risible level of nurses' remuneration meant that patient confidentiality was often only a fig leaf which could be brushed aside with cash.

Information trickled into Ganesh's email address.

Three correspondents could recall the nursing home, each with a different name for director or chief medical officer.

All claimed the reward. Only one collected.

The victor was a certain Miss. Nicholls; a grasping Lancashire accent who, on confirmation of her money, would provide a name and telephone number for a doctor who had been the Nursing Home's consultant during the relevant period.

Ganesh had only once fallen for this trick. It had been as a schoolboy in London.

He informed his Midlands matriarch that her money would be placed in an escrow account, accessible only by a firm of solicitors beyond reproach.

She should furnish them with her information. They would verify or otherwise its validity and, all being well, release the funds to her.

Miss. Nicholls could only agree; she could see that her unlooked for benefactor was unlikely to yield to the price hike she had had in mind.

The telephone number belonged to a Professor John Ramsay, senior and revered orthopaedic surgeon now retired for more than ten years.

That there was nothing decrepit about Prof. Ramsay's memory was immediately obvious to Ganesh. He could sense the keen intellect and listen to the carefully chosen answers to his preliminary introduction and questions.

A telephone call, he knew, would not do. There was a gentleman in the old-fashioned sense at the other end of the line.

Old world rules applied; face to face it would have to be. The professor's choice, Ganesh's wallet, but where exactly was Peebles?

Prof. Ramsay was early at the Spa Hotel.

He had passed an enjoyable morning selecting a puppy from an eight week old litter of Cocker Spaniels and felt he merited the large gin that he had before him.

He looked with satisfaction at the shabby splendour of the sitting room; it would hardly be, he thought, what this private eye fellow was expecting.

The food also was hardly London best although the wine list, really rather good.

He still did not know how much to reveal. The question had been simple enough. Did he recall or know a Miss. Turnbull from his Glasgow days?

He had replied, cautiously, that he might. He would consult his records and memory. The result, if any, he would divulge on meeting.

In reality he had no need of records, his memory was excellent and while his recollection of Glasgow days was hazy, he had seen Miss. Turnbull since. Not often it was true, but...

Scotland is a small place and he knew her story, knew her foibles, had known her employer and her daughter; he even knew where she was buried.

Professor Ramsay, Ganesh learned, had been Matthew's surgeon.

His legs, terribly mangled during the war, had been a constant irritation to him and an equally constant source of income for the Scottish orthopaedic profession.

Prof. Ramsay had come to know Matthew and admire the stoicism with which he bore his pain.

Friendship had been born; Ramsay was a younger son and frustrated farmer. The hill at Gladdies with its smattering of grouse and hidden loch was an ideal place to work his spaniels and forget the smell of ether and antiseptic.

He had not been a frequent visitor but had come often enough to get re-acquainted with Miss. Turnbull and to note that somewhere along the way she had acquired a pretty and vivacious daughter.

At Matthew's funeral he had, despite the heavy rain and poisonous atmosphere, noted a Turnbull headstone alongside the freshly dug grave.

Not that there was anything odd about this, he told Ganesh; the cemetery was small and space at a premium.

The daughter had been there but he did not recall seeing her at the wake and that was that.

His information spent, Ramsay sat back with an expectant look, but like the medical profession, Ganesh kept his secrets close and there was really nothing further to say.

Chapter 17

It was to an ailing old lady that Ganesh made his report.

Alice had inherited the high blood pressure and poor circulation of her father.

It had killed him with one massive coronary. It was killing her by a series of small, debilitating strokes.

To her closest friends and she had confided in very few, it seemed that the search for her lost child and the hope that this engendered, was the mainspring of her life. Her last reserve of energy.

Alice had managed, almost, to convince herself that the search was pointless. In any event, why would a child make time for a mother who had had clearly none for it?

It was a shock, therefore, when Ganesh telephoned with his news.

Shocks, even those of pleasure, are not good for old, overstrained hearts and she was increasingly breathless as she waited for written confirmation and fuller detail.

A private nurse and her closest friend were with her when the letter came. Both agreed on the point and time of crisis.

She had been reading aloud, slowly but firmly until she said the word 'Gladdies'.

A look of blank incomprehension had come over her face; then tears.

Shaking, sobbing inconsolable tears.

There was no seizure in the classic style but it proved to be the fit that eventually killed her.

Her friends rallied around, but she seemed to know that time was short and there was one last task to perform. Sir Merlin and his Jersey-based acolyte were summoned. Alice received them in her bedroom. Offers of support from well-meaning and frankly curious friends were declined.

It was a mistake.

Her speech may have been slurred but her head was clear and finally her life had meaning.

It was a pale and tight lipped London lawyer who emerged from the room, but a grimly satisfied one who returned the next day.

It was the last time that Sir Merlin ever saw Alice.

She died shortly after, save for a dog, alone as always, in her sleep.

In herself, however, Alice had never felt less alone.

Matthew had not totally abandoned her. It could not be coincidence that their child had grown up in his house.

What had he told her? Anything or nothing? Why had he not told Alice?

She was not religious, but as often happens at the end of life, bets are hedged and the possibility of a God reviewed anew.

Perhaps she would be soon reunited with Matthew and her long lost daughter. She hoped so.

While Alice had left Jersey calm and happier than when she had arrived, the same could not be said of Sir Merlin. A will had been rewritten. It had been, legally, simple enough and the reason for haste obvious.

This wretched girl, whose very existence he often privately doubted, was one step closer to reality. If she could be found she might, and he used that word advisedly, inherit.

If not, various charities would benefit.

Sir Merlin as executor and sole trustee had firm ideas concerning charity.

For him, charity began at home.

He would not try too hard in his search for this hidden beneficiary: and muddled old women often make curious choices where a will is concerned.

Chapter 18

The brusque command left by Spender on Joy's answer phone spoke of urgency. Her response lacked it.

There was no doubt that Spender possessed charm, it was just that he did not waste it on friends.

Thus, the order to read her email was nothing exceptional. Probably, he merely wanted confirmation or otherwise of some item of salacious gossip.

It intrigued her that Johnny Laidlaw was also involved.

Perhaps the subject matter related to Cambridge days or perhaps Spender had recently graced the Border country with his presence, something he had been known to do if the invitation was good enough.

Those from Johnny certainly fell into this category.

Apart from that, she doubted that they met much. Johnny was not really town and Spender required lavish entertainment to risk rural discomfort.

Returning to her screen with a cup of coffee, Joy noted the unopened envelope signs with resignation. There were many. Mainly unsolicited offers of things she neither needed nor wanted.

It did not help that her husband, being a technophobe, used her email address on the rare occasions he needed the Internet.

Slowly she worked down the list, opening and deleting, until she was left with just two. Spender and Laidlaw: she chose Johnny first.

'Joy, hope you're well, raining here as ever. I've been contacted by some lawyer wallah from Edinburgh. Wanted to talk about you. Dry old stick, wouldn't say much; hoped to get your contact details, about which, of course, I kept mum.

It is, I'm sure, coincidence but the wraith like lady who now lives at Gladdies has been sounding off a bit of late.

Claims that you're a cross between the Pink Panther and Pol Pot. Obviously hasn't looked in the mirror recently.

Needless to say, no one pays much attention.

Told the old fellow, called Joffrey by the way, that I would try and contact you. Hope you don't mind.

Get in touch it's been ages.

Oodles and oodles, Johnny.'

Joy read this message with growing unease. It was no surprise to hear that Petronella was denigrating her. There had never been a time when this was not the case. It was sweet of Johnny to say that no one heeded her, but his mere mention of the fact meant that her lies must be more specific than usual.

Then there was the lawyer, Joffrey. She had long expected and always dreaded this day.

The old walnut silver canteen that had meant so much to Matthew.

She could not understand the contents but evidently someone else did. They were theirs and they wanted them back.

She had not dared, indeed been too upset, to open the box until safely back in London.

She had not told her soldier husband of its existence nor its contents.

The only person alive who knew its secrets was her second and, she hoped, last husband. But it must be because of the box that a Scottish solicitor was looking for her and she could well imagine Petronella stirring the pot.

In these days of astronomic city bonuses £100,000 may seem small beer. For a housekeeper's daughter in her early twenties it had been a small fortune.

It spelt independence.

It apologised for hard and selfish women but most of all it spoke of love.

Joy had been stunned, quite literally unable to move.

The biggest banknote she had ever seen before this was £50 and then very infrequently. Here there were two rolls of them neatly wound with an elastic band and a small typed sheet which simply stated £100,000 in denominations of £50.

There were also letters and photographs.

They all dated to a time before Joy's birth and, she realised, before Matthew had been married.

One name occurred more often than the rest, 'Alice'.

Whether she featured in the photographs Joy could not say, nor did Alice appear to have a surname, however it was evident that she and Matthew had been lovers.

Something terrible must have happened, she thought, for him to have ended up with Andrea rather than Alice.

Joy made a conscious effort to stop her reverie.

She had always wondered if Matthew's present would one day return to haunt her. It was long since spent and paying it back would mean selling something, probably something precious.

While life at Gladdies had been comfortable, Matthew had never been expansive with money; any surplus went to Andrea.

In theory he could, she supposed, give what he wanted to whom he liked, but she was merely a servant's child.

The gift was in anonymous cash and there was no covering letter, no evidence to prove that it had been freely given rather than taken.

She could well imagine an unexplained withdrawal from a bank account coinciding with her visit to Gladdies.

It did not need Petronella's twisted imagination for two and two to make four.

She turned to Spender's email. Perhaps she would need his professional help.

It turned out to be the opposite.

What had Joy done, he asked, so terrible that thinly veiled threats were made to reveal her whereabouts?

Montmorillon had been put at risk.

His integrity as a barrister questioned.

No less than a prince of the legal world, Bencher and member of the Bar Council was digging.

If someone could afford those fees, only to squander this precious time on elementary groundwork, Joy must have ruffled some very expensive feathers indeed.

He needed answers now.

Had it not been for her own uneasy conscience Joy would have found nothing untoward in Spender's words.

He did not tolerate fools, let alone gladly and there were many he found, by his own high standards, foolish.

These had included, at various times, most friends, usually his family and always those in positions senior to him. They suffered, he said, from altitude sickness and he had often made it his business to point this fact out.

From experience she knew that these crises of alarm and despondency did not last long. Spender was not given to introspection, action was his forte, often along lines as alarming to his allies as to his enemies.

Nonetheless she would ring him and smooth the creases if they were still there.

Flattery sometimes worked but he was too intelligent to be much influenced by such verbal pomade.

In any case, he often considered it to be not far off the mark.

He did not pick up and nor did Joy expect him to. She knew that he used his answering machine as a preliminary filter for disappointed creditors, angry ladies and, always, his brother. She had seen the procedure often enough. The most frequent callers were displayed in full colour on his mobile screen.

Maybe he was abroad; the frequent flyer attending to his diverse portfolio of commercial projects.

The Congo, she recalled, was a new favourite, its combination of bribeability and extreme lawlessness appealing to his lawyers mind.

As it turned out he was not in Africa but the staider environment of Guernsey.

Thanks to Joy, he said, he had been obliged to visit one of his many bankers, Royal Trust Company of some Antillean island so small that Joy had never even heard of it.

It was a nuisance but he, with difficulty, could spare a couple of days.

It was well-known that farmers did nothing, he therefore proposed to catch a ferry to St Malo where she could pick him up.

While he was with them he would like to see Louis again, a dinner party would be fun. She should book him a return flight to London three days hence, from the local airport. Unless he heard to the country he would see her tomorrow.

Oh, and bring the green car, the other one disagreed with his back.

It was obvious to Joy that the crisis had passed and that the Spender world had resumed its complicated orbit.

She, no less than her husband, adored him and she really did want to speak.

He had effortlessly extracted himself from many worse situations than the one she currently occupied and financial skulduggery always put him on his mettle.

However, St Malo was a good five hours drive away and she, or her husband, would need to make an early start.

The latter she knew, would offer. He could pass the outward hours with his terrible 1970s music, a taste Spender shared, and the return journey would allow them to recount their earlier ventures; stories that she had heard so many times she felt she had almost been there.

It was a ritual between them, unavoidable and better got over with as soon as possible, preferably alone.

She went to break the news to the small fat man clipping box hedges in the sun.

Part Two

Chapter 19

The man Joy sought, her husband, was called Mick Bouleau.

He had been married to her for some twenty five years and had known Spender for as long as he could remember.

He was small, stocky and running to fat.

What had once been a fine head of hair, parted centrally in the 70s style, was retreating sideways and backwards.

His head was often topped by a pair of rimless spectacles of the type known to Spender as 'German homosexual'.

His attire was shabby; tatty shorts and cheap patterned shirts, although, should the occasion warrant, he could scrub up reasonably well.

He considered himself an uncomplicated, down to earth, man.

'Thick' was the term Spender used.

At home in a rural setting, much less so when in town.

Although the bearer of a British passport he had never lived there, save for brief sojourns at school and university.

His parents had emigrated to Rhodesia at the end of the second war seeking a better climate and food that was not rationed. Both had served their country in that conflict, spending a part of their youth in less than carefree pursuits and colonial Africa seemed like heaven.

They had not known each other before. He had jumped at the chance to be ADC to the new Governor General, a distant relation.

She was making an extended visit to her uncle, one of the vanishing breed of white hunter explorers.

For her it was the tranquillity of a hidden valley, cocooned in the Eastern Highlands hard by the border of Mozambique. For him, the bustle and social whirl of Government House in the capital, Salisbury.

He was a handsome man, resplendent in tropical whites; she a shy, dark haired beauty. Nature had taken its course and armed with a magnificent dowry from the childless uncle, a plot of land had been purchased near the small farming town of Karoi.

It was here that Mick was conceived and born, closely followed by three sisters and a brother who had died in childbirth.

His parents had built a house in the colonial style . It was long, low and rambling as rooms were added to accommodate children and guests.

The main feature was a wide verandah that ran the length of the building on its western façade. This was comfortably furnished with tables, chairs, sofas and dog beds. Blinds could be drawn against sun or wind and a section, the nursery, was fly screened although mosquito nets still had to be used at night.

A long and dusty drive wound up to the house from the main Salisbury, Kariba Road. Then down again behind the small hill on which the house was situated, to the farm buildings and compound where the labour force lived.

In time, Mick's mother had opened a small store selling basic foodstuffs, sweets and cheap clothes. There was a tiny primary school and a corrugated iron chapel built on stilts against the termites which doubled as a surgery without doctor and, several times a year, cinema.

The family had been, to the childish mind of Mick, like an ocean liner. Self-contained and self-sufficient with little contact to the wider world. Reflecting now on those childish impressions, Mick knew them to be ridiculous; but then, at that age, he had never seen the sea.

The farm was not initially productive. Neither of Mick's parents had an agricultural background and the location had been selected more for looks than fertility.

It is a strange but common conceit among men leaving the military that, having been officers, they will be able to farm.

They have visions of commanding an obedient workforce by means of morning parades and verbal orders. The rest of the day can be used in sporting pursuits with the occasional inspection thrown in to keep everyone on their toes.

The ample evidence that this method does not work is compensated for by military energy and complicated planning. Special skills are thought either not necessary or easily acquired along the way.

Their new neighbours despite, in European terms, being far away, watched with interest. They were an eclectic mixture of tough efficient Afrikaners and eccentric Britons now by two or even three generations Rhodesian.

What they shared was an ability to turn bush into farmland and wrest a living from an unforgiving environment.

They knew the farm, Berry Hills, with its thin soil and lack of water. They had watched the two previous owners come, fail and leave.

Given a price of half what the Bouleaus had paid, they might have even bid for it themselves.

They did not expect to have to wait too long for their next opportunity.

Mick's father was not sufficiently stubborn to give them that satisfaction.

A more determined type of man would have met failure with yet more energy, only stopping when the purse was empty.

James Bouleau realised within the first years that he preferred the romance of the bush on celluloid and, if possible, in an air-conditioned cinema.

He had a gentle, almost effeminate, nature which privately recoiled from the tough efficiency needed to prosper in that environment. In short, he was not made for physical labour.

While no intellectual, he was intelligent, quick on the uptake and very good with almost everyone except the type of man who were now his neighbours.

Farming bored him, Karoi society bored him, and while he loved his wife and children, they alone could not provide sufficient stimulus to hold him in the bush.

He became a weekly commuter to Salisbury.

Mick's mother took intermittent marriage in her stride. She was an undemonstrative woman but possessed the hard core that her husband lacked. She loved the African space, the heat, the violent thunderstorms and myriad variety of insects, plants, birds and animals. Luckily, she was also richer than her husband which lent persuasion to her argument for retaining the farm.

With her husband safely in town for much of the time she began to receive visits from the local bachelors and married men alike. It was not her of whom they had been wary. Offers of help were followed by action.

Scrub was cleared, a dam site proposed and pure bred cattle exchanged for disease resistant native hybrids.

There had been, initially, talk of a manager to run the place and, with luck and hard work, that might one day be possible.

For the present, a system of neighbourly know-how in exchange for a share of any profit had to suffice and a viable farm slowly took shape.

The farm was paradise for a small boy such as Mick.

He grew fast, indeed was big for his age.

His mother's aged nanny had been summoned from England to lend an air of sobriety and discipline to the nursery.

She did not last.

Africa was simply too foreign for her and the creepy-crawlies too big.

Faith, a lady who by her diminutive stature and bronzed skin, betrayed a Bushman heritage was engaged.

Apart from the native Shona she could also speak in a language of clicks and whistles, something close to nature itself.

She came with a son, Gideon, just one year older than Mick. In a world of sisters he became an older brother and Mick's cultural landscape moved steadily away from the European model to a world of animism where birds and animals had their own stories.

The regime of shoes, shirts and hats was the next to wither.

Mick's mother was too busy on the farm to correct each infringement and Faith, in private, thought the rules silly.

Shona became Mick's daily tongue. English was reserved,

like French with the Russian aristocracy, for formal occasions when people came to visit.

His father did not approve but could hardly feign surprise. Absentee figureheads are either worshipped or ignored; he fell into the latter category.

Education was rudimentary, a mixture of farm school, self-help and liberal doses of the Bible.

An inquisitive mind led Mick to books. Kipling and Willard Price were favourites. French also made an early showing with Tintin in the original. His mother, wisely, guarded the English versions as an aide- memoire when her knowledge failed.

His real forte, however, was the world outside. By the age of seven he was on intimate terms with the local environment. The imitations that he saw hanging on the walls indoors paled next to the vibrancy of the original.

Inevitably this happy ignorance of the twentieth century could not last. While both parents admired the theory of the noble savage, they knew that their son would need more to succeed in a modern world.

A Salisbury school was selected, boarding, with the other boys in long smelly dormitories. The curriculum was British, the ethos Rhodesian and the emphasis, muscular.

Mick hated it. He was as alien to his new colleagues as they, being mainly urban boys, were to him.

When he spoke English it was with the accent of Europe not Africa; cue ridicule.

Only the gardeners spoke Shona and his mastery of that language led to resentment and even harsher verdicts.

The other boys, if at all, knew only Kitchen Kaffir, that bastardised language of the white memsahibs.

They neither liked nor trusted him and so the standard behaviour of group to outsider began. At school it is called bullying.

Luckily he was stubborn.

Neither the half drownings at swimming nor the orchestrated pummelling on the rugby pitch led to capitulation.

He was not deaf and soon realised that his father was not universally admired in the tight little world of white Salisbury.

It was logical that the son should be tarred with the same liberal brush.

He did not seek help from the teachers, he knew it was not there.

This self containment increased his isolation but gained a grudging respect. The bullies never stopped, but a pig that does not squeal is less exciting than one that does and there were always other victims.

It was around this time that Spender came into his life.

Their fathers had known each other during the war and kept, vaguely, in touch.

Mr Spender senior was obliged to visit Rhodesia on behalf of his employers, Lloyds.

He took the opportunity for a family safari and a little polo. His wife's protests about what she called the Sergeants Mess of Africa fell on deaf ears.

Since when, he asked, had Sergeants been underwriting polo players?

Overall the holiday had been a success, the week at Berry Hills, less so. However, a friendship had developed between the sons, Saville and Mick.

An attraction of opposites.

For Mick it was a relief to meet a white boy with the same accent as him and someone with a sense of humour not only involving pain.

Chapter 20

As he grew the political situation deteriorated.

UDI, the unilateral declaration of independence, came in 1965.

For the children this simply meant the unavailability of certain brands of sweets and cereals. Sanctions bit harder on the adult world and opinions became more polarised. More, literally, black and white.

Among the educated African cadre there were those who despaired of universal suffrage and true democracy. They looked for another solution.

To the east and west the Portuguese colonies, aided by an ever helpful Soviet hand, led by example.

Zambia, to the north, freed from colonial shackles provided sanctuary.

The English left offered supporting words.

The insurgency started.

At first it was a matter of isolated attacks on isolated farms. It soon became nastier.

It was against this background that Mick's parents took their decision. They had both fought for a cause that seemed not only just, but imperative.

Victory, if at times unlikely, had always been possible.

For them, this coming war had all the hallmarks of zealotry and any outcome was likely to be worse than the status quo.

A general draft for all white young men was already being considered, along with much bellicose propaganda. It was true that there were excellent public schools in the country, but an English education was something they had long debated and this provided the spur.

Like many men who have not been there, Bouleau's father had a complicated attitude towards Eton College. Bits of him hated the smug assurance of their alumni; most of him envied it.

In the era before the tyranny of league tables such rarefied establishments were attainable, even from an African starting point. Learning was something to be built on potential. The pre-polished article was not, then, essential.

Thus it was that Mick became a stiff collared, tail suited English schoolboy. It was not to his liking. He was again an outsider but his chameleon facility with accent and a robust physique ensured that he stuck.

British bullying could not compare with the Southern Hemisphere variety and Rhodesian rugby had been a harder school than the famous playing fields he now graced.

Like many before him, he found sanctuary in sport and with success came acceptance.

Holidays were spent with grandmothers and an eccentric collection of great aunts.

He learned to drink, smoke and charm his elders.

The Spender house was a frequent refuge in winter while the long summer break meant a return to Africa.

To general surprise exams were passed. Success has a happy habit of self perpetuation and all seemed set fair until one disastrous night in early December 1975.

Chimurenga, the liberation war, came to Berry Hills. Mick was in England, the rest of his family at home.

By morning they had become another sad statistic on a fast growing list.

The eight foot security fence topped with razor wire, the dogs, the command detonated grenades concealed among the frangipani and hibiscus, even the last resort FN rifle; none stopped the human wave of hatred.

All that the security forces could do on arrival was treat a tortured and brutalised workforce, sift the charred embers for clues, and put bodies into bags.

Another small island of enlightenment had been carelessly extinguished along the road to a dubious and selective freedom.

The news that he was an orphan and sole proprietor of a heavily mortgaged piece of Africa did not reach Mick quickly.

Neighbours and friends had their own safety to look to first and there was a natural reluctance to be the bearer of such catastrophic information.

'Eventually, it was left to a combination of the family solicitor in Salisbury to impart the legal implications and neighbours, the von Seidels, the emotional.

Both letters arrived with Mick's paternal grandmother, a stern but practical lady. She had read such missives before. Two brothers in the first war and a husband in the second. Now a son and all his family save the boy, her grandson, of whom ,despite old-fashioned formality, she approved.

Her class and generation were strangers to prevarication. She placed a telephone call and the next day drove her ancient Morris to Eton, realising that her presence was needed to lend backbone to a horrified house master, ordered to break the news.

Mick received the summons to his tutors study without qualms. It was not an unusual event and his conscience was clear.

The audience revealed as he opened the door changed all that. His house master, his Dame, the house matron, the college chaplain but most of all his grandmother and the set of her face, told him why he was here.

It was a day that he had half expected.

He read the newspapers with their dry reports. His mother's letters said the same thing but in colour. She had even hinted of a temporary evacuation.

It seemed that she was too late.

It was not the fact of tragedy but its totality that was the surprise, the awkward diction of his house master and the writhing of the chaplain's hands underlining the finality of his sentence.

Lunch with his grandmother was an awkward silence.

She did not cry so neither did he.

What was done could not be undone.

'Routine is balm', she said and routine was school. He was coming to her for Christmas in any case, a week or so hence. Emotion, she stated, was something to be done in private.

'Be strong, wait for Christmas'.

In an enclosed society news is currency, bad news more valuable than good and calamity the best of all. The sideways, sympathetic look on his teachers faces spoke of a breach of his secret but he was too numb to care.

Some boys also seemed to know; the chaplain he supposed but he kept his grandmother's counsel and said nothing.

There was one exception. He told Spender, he knew it would go no further.

Chapter 21

Christmas was not jolly but his grandmother had a well tested recipe for grief.

Planning.

Nothing too distant, attainable goals.

They agreed that there was nothing to be gained by an early visit to Berry Hills. It would be managed, as far as was possible, by the neighbours.

In the meantime Mick would concentrate on his work. Depending on exam results and if he was still so minded, he could return with the near certainty of military call-up which was what he secretly wanted.

A memorial service was held in the little Surrey village to where the old lady had retired. What family was left to him came and offered platitudes and promises. A bleak New Year was seen in. Then it was back to school.

When one's present and one's past are so abruptly erased only the future remains. It is possible to slump into gloomy introspective contemplation of what might have been but even Mick could see that this was a pointless cul-de-sac.

He was not rich and his prospects were slim. He was, however, a son of the Southern Hemisphere.

There had never been much charity for a European in Africa.

If something was needed, it was self-help and hard work. If not, it didn't happen.

It was thus he rationalised his position to himself.

In his case, this meant getting qualifications first, then back home and make things right.

His grandmother had said she would pay until A-levels. Beyond that, who knew?

He was a latter day voortrekker; push on, salvation is over the next line of hills.

Chapter 22

Focus is a potent force.

Certainly this seemed the case to Mick's gratified tutors.

He was no academic and the results he gained were the product of battery not brilliance. They were, nonetheless, sufficient to try for Cambridge.

It helped that he had followed Spender to the river. He was not the right shape for an oarsman but in a small pond determination goes a long way and a seat in the Eton Eight has been known to tip the scales with aquatically minded colleges.

Mick's gain was Westminster College's loss. He would take neither Blue nor First but that was for the future.

The present faced him with a dilemma and he sought advice.

His grandmother.

She did not hold with dilemmas.

She quickly extracted two promises backed by fiscal threat.

The first was to accept his place at Cambridge. The second was not to cross Rhodesian boundaries until the war, then entering its final struggle, was over.

He loved his grandmother and realised that any disobedience, when combined with her emphysema, the product of a lifetime's devotion to Players Navy Cut and Scotch would probably kill her.

His Gap year came thanks to Spender.

Improbably, given his patrician bearing, Spender had American blood. Rich American blood.

The first stage of a seven month odyssey was an uncomfortable working crossing of the Atlantic on a Cunard container ship. More Spender cousins.

Their arrival in New York was also less than serene. They had negotiated a hot and hostile subway to Grand Central Station before the volcano blew.

Even now, Mick found it astonishing to remember how fast a rush hour crowd had parted under the waves of Anglo-Saxon oaths aimed at him by an enraged Spender.

For two months their ways had parted.

Spender went to impart aquatic wisdom to privileged boys at an exclusive school on the Hudson River.

Mick helped to teach sixth grade in suburban Connecticut.

He lived with Spender's aunt, a charming and bohemian divorcee with a household of mongrels.

All seemed well until the fall came in the shape of a letter from England.

It was addressed to the aunt, but since it concerned him, she shared the contents with Mick.

They were not flattering and dealt in detail with his antecedents, ability and prospects. The aunt found it funny, Mick less so, although he could not fault the perception of the author, the aunt's sister. It was a salutary reminder that he had a long way to go.

The remaining months in America were spent together, moving West. Travel was by Greyhound bus, the first and last time in his life that Spender used such a mode of transport.

He preferred taxis he said.

Jobs were various and short. Sometimes with outlying branches of

Spenderdom, sometimes not.

Eventually they arrived in San Francisco where they parted; Mick home to bury his grandmother, Spender on a triumphal tour of Canada. More relations.

Their friendship, already close, had been welded by shared experience.

Hardship, as Spender would later claim.

But everything is relative and one man's mansion is another's slum.

Chapter 23

Cambridge had been fun. Mick's circle widened somewhat without ever straying too far from the Cam.

Rhodesia/Zimbabwe was the spectre at the feast, the end to present means.

His first two years passed quickly, lazily productive but with no high note. It took his third and final year to inject urgency.

Part of this, as for all idle undergraduates, was the looming imminence of finals.

Part was love.

A girl, blonde and noisy, friend of Johnny Laidlaw and as happily uncomplicated as he. Joy.

Mick could only applaud from the touchline. It was common knowledge that she was spoken for. In any case, what could he offer?

Nonetheless, he could hope and, given will power, wait. She appeared to know who he was and seemed to enjoy his company, although that was true for a host of others.

In any case, he would soon be beyond reach in the hopeful dawn of the newly independent multicultural infant state of Zimbabwe.

Given its current parlous situation, it is easy to forget the bright optimism that then prevailed in Zimbabwe.

Reconciliation and a heartfelt desire to make things work were the focus. The war had been long enough and bitter enough that those whites still remaining were committed.

True, there were some ominous pointers for the future, most notably the genocidal campaign by President Robert Mugabe's North Korean trained fifth Brigade against his erstwhile comrades, the Ndebele, in the south.

Commercial farming though, had a future.

The new government had stated it clearly.

Spare land, abandoned during the war, was to be acquired, distributed or sold.

A market economy, or near enough, reigned and the agricultural machine moved up through the gears.

There were profits to be made and eager customers to the north, west and east, they having destroyed their own infrastructures.

It was to this country that Mick came 'home'.

After eight years in exile with an English education behind him, it was an odd experience.

Some things had not changed.

Immediately, there was that unique smell of Africa; faintly acrid, composed of wood smoke and sweat.

There were the sights and sounds of the bush, not coffee table safari, but the small intimate things that only one who has grown up with them notices.

People and places, however, were different.

The former, either dead, departed or harder, less easy-going: brittle.

The latter, either brutally functional or dilapidated.

Overall was that sense of diminution always experienced when childhood memories are revisited with adult eyes.

For all that, he was back where he wanted and there was much to do.

The current custodian of Berry Hills was a neighbour some thirty minutes distant, Murdo MacDonald Murray.

Mick had hardly known the family; he had been thirteen when he left after all, but there had been an intermittent correspondence with his grandmother. She had called them saints. She had been, as usual, right.

Murdo was a small, stringy man burnt by decades of African sun, such that his eyes seemed a startling blue. His energy and good humour were evident from first acquaintance.

His own farm bore witness to his competence.

To this busy world Mick could bring little, save rusty Shona and a hunger to learn.

In an expanding scene it was enough and his labour paid for knowledge gained.

Berry Hills, never much developed, was as good as derelict.

The house was a ruin, burnt on that infamous night and left to rot with its ghosts.

Several small rondavels for the farmhands had been built in the garden and those few fields with irrigation were still cultivated. The livestock had gone. It was not an encouraging sight.

With a gentle wisdom born of many disappointments Murdo deflected any detailed discussions of the future. He concentrated on teaching and the slow process of re-assimilation. The boy was intelligent, he reasoned, and would work out for himself that the farm was not viable now and probably never had been.

In the meantime Mick was dispatched on an agricultural Grand Tour. He helped with maize in the Midlands. Forestry and tea in the Eastern Highlands. Cattle in the south and game farming in the North and West. It took three years. It owed nothing to Eton or Cambridge save an ability to reason, but it left him, if still broke, able to offer some rudimentary skills to a future employer.

While money was tight in the southern half of Africa, the opposite was true in the booming Thatcherite London of the 1980s.

The newly deregulated city was awash with deals, the entire world flooding in, and almost anyone, it seemed, could ride this wave.

Never a disciple of follow the crowd, Spender chose to lead.

He chose ice cream.

Many a fad, he thought, had its roots in America. Simply pick the latest and translate to London before anyone else.

It was a sound principle and there was money to spare for his tiny handmade tubs with pretentious names.

The raw material, milk, was cheap and the chi-chi delicatessens of the SW milieu sold out as fast as they could stock.

It was, as Spender modestly pronounced when interviewed for the Sunday colour supplements, a triumph.

Sadly, business is like war and one triumph may not

necessarily mean a campaign won. War and trade need leaders but they must also have managers. Spender was aware of this and, as he was clearly the former, he hired the latter.

The heady combination of adulation, to which he was used and a lot of ready money, to which he was not, deflected his focus sufficiently to let in the financial bazaar.

Where Spender saw flats and Ferraris they saw empire. Good branding, poor funding and a world of shelves waiting to be filled. They also had that most useful item, a cuckoo in the nest; the manager.

A generous offer was made together with the observation that one cannot patent ice cream.

Spender had no real choice, despite noisy protest, other than to accept. In any case, he was already becoming bored by ice cream. He liked nightclubs; why not buy one? He would still have cash to spare.

Thus it was that Mick found himself the surprised recipient of an invitation to ski. Accommodation found, travel not.

He had never been skiing. Indeed he had not been back to Europe since coming down from Cambridge. The lure of crisp white cold as a change from heat, flies and dust was undeniable. A free pass from Spender a very rare item, but what really clinched his decision was one of the fellow invitees. Joy.

The holiday had mixed results. Skiing was not as easy as it looked and his host's patience, never his forte, was at times severely tested.

It did not help that Johnny Laidlaw was clearly superior.

Luckily for Mick, Joy too was a novice and the time spent slowly snow ploughing together rekindled their former friendship.

Her soldier and she had parted, he learned.

A change of air seemed wise.

A trip to Zimbabwe was proposed, agonised over and finally accepted.

The ability to paint is a transferable skill and if Mick rather oversold the opportunities of a burgeoning Harare, it was to a willing buyer and he felt no guilt.

Chapter 24

On first acquaintance, Africa takes different people in different ways.

For Mick it was home, the bush beyond criticism and town sufficiently small to be acceptable.

The seamier political side was simply a fact of life.

Most Europeans, out to watch game from exclusive lodges, held similar views.

Joy built her impressions from a different base. India.

Given her earlier and extensive wanderings in the subcontinent, Mick could not fault her observation.

Superficially there were similarities; heat and an alien smell.

Nature also was extravagant in its diversity and opulence, so that sometimes, when she shut her eyes, she could imagine herself back in the Western Ghats or Maharashtra plain.

However, she only had to open them for India to fall away.

Here there was no culture.

No network of ancient towns and villages, no palaces or temples. She missed the throng of noisy, busy people, engaged in hectic commerce, odd devotion or argument.

The land seemed empty, a shimmering heat haze that followed an unused tarmac strip to the horizon.

Urban architecture was crumbling colonial, rapidly ceding to American high-rise. Rural was planter bungalow, African rondavel or tin shack commerce, but they were so few and so far apart.

Even the people, black or white, seemed uniform in attire and outlook.

Here the human footprint was as faint as the wild world was clear.

Still, it was not London and the Penalonga Valley where Mick was currently based, rolling and beautiful.

It was obvious from the start that Joy did not share Mick's

unblinking enthusiasm for her new environment. It was one of her traits that he loved, an inability to dissemble.

Never said unkindly, simply a neutral fact.

He knew that she was a country girl through and through. He had not appreciated that she might not be a wilderness girl, and that from time to time the pavement would beckon.

Several months passed. The grandest hotel in Mutare, the nearest town, became the proud owner of a panelled sitting room, complete with marble lobby; this in a country where the real thing was probably cheaper than Joy's rates.

In the absence of competition, Mick's attention and proposals became more compelling. He dared to dream of the future.

That it would not involve Berry Hills he accepted, albeit sadly.

He suspected that any future probably did not include Zimbabwe either.

Despite the anguish of choosing between two loves, if she would have him he would follow.

Chapter 25

The wedding was, in Spender's view, rustic.

Neither had family to attend. Friends were at the other end of prohibitive airfares.

Worse still, much of his elegantly crafted speech was lost on the small gathering of awkwardly suited farmers.

The local Semanje-manje band was, however, acceptable and the meat on the wedding brai, barbecue to him, very good.

He was less complimentary about the locally produced champagne, but in this he was not alone.

A honeymoon was taken on the Mozambique coast. It was short and basic. That unfortunate country's infrastructure was struggling to rebuild after the devastation of civil war. Even if they had been able to afford one, hotels were few and uncomfortable. A tent had sufficed.

But the warmth of the Indian Ocean could not totally dispel that feeling of shock common to many newly- weds. Uncertainty for the future and panic for the past, with bridges truly burned by the words'I do'.

They survived. It was now time for long-term planning.

Step one was about capital, currently non-existent.

Berry Hills must be sold; a task as difficult emotionally as practically.

It was offered to the Government and rejected, although it would be later confiscated from its new proprietors by those same politicians, accusing them of colonial pillage. Eventually the long suffering neighbours were persuaded.

For them, this was more charity than any business logic.

The amount raised was not impressive.

Stage two was easier. The what?

Farming for him: painting for her and all hands firmly touching wood.

It was number three that posed the real problem.

Where?

The traditional escape routes for fleeing Zimbabweans, those taking 'the gap', followed a well trodden Antipodean, Canadian or South African path.

The more adventurous or less well-heeled, went north or west to their broken neighbours where they found their agricultural acumen increasingly in demand.

While the latter appealed to Mick it seemed more of the same to Joy and was quickly vetoed.

Money and climate meant that Britain was out of the question and Joy, with the private guilt of her secret walnut box shunned proximity to Scotland. The remainder of First World options were also too expensive.

This process of reduction pointed inextricably to Europe; be it Latin, Iberian or French. Spain was rejected by Joy on linguistic grounds; she favoured the land of fresco. Farming, however, would remain their main source of income and the lure of cheap land allied to the shaky basis of a French O level, pulled them north.

All disagreement on their choice had been settled by that very rare bird; French initiative. The national young farmer scheme.

Chapter 26

France was then and remains still, deeply attached to its agricultural roots. The Code Napoleon is largely responsible.

There are few Parisians, Bordeaulais or Lyonnais who would not claim a link to the land. Very often they are co-owners of slowly diminishing hectares.

This does not mean that they have any active desire to work their plot, rather it is an emotional attachment to the ideal of the noble paysan.

In any case, they often cannot reach agreement in respect of a sale. Add to this, the reluctance of French youth to toil for small reward when they could be warm and dry behind a computer screen, and you have the ingredients for a Gallic crise.

The solution arrived at was simple and effective. Young farmers, not only French but from throughout the European Union, would be helped.

To qualify one needed to be under forty years old, hold some relevant qualification, degree or diploma, and have a minimum, very little, level of capital.

Aid would be given in the acquisition, stocking and management of the new farm, via direct subsidy and ten-year interest-free loans.

For the young Bouleau couple it was too good to ignore. Any other solution meant a surrender of independence and a salaried job, if indeed one could be found. Mick qualified thanks to his British passport and various certificates gained from Zimbabwean courses.

It was different. A shot in the dark, but they had very little to lose and, potentially, a life to gain.

The start, Joy recalled, had seemed endless. She had lodged with Spender again, hoping to profit from London's current insatiable appetite for paint effects.

Mick had taken work where he could find it, usually as a relief milker on West Country dairy farms.

There was neither time nor money for the social whirl and their presence went largely unnoticed.

The high and sometimes low points came with the regular visits to France to view the properties proposed by the French government agency, Safer.

They were pushed towards milk, market gardening or pigs. None appealed.

Both came from a more open, extensive, type of agriculture.

Eventually the French relented and concentrated more on livestock: sheep and cattle.

Beggars cannot be choosers and grazing animals need grass.

A combination of poverty and climatic imperative pushed them towards the hilly and impoverished centre of France .

La France profonde where many a bourgeoise claimed his heart lay, while not actually deigning to live there.

It was the Limousin where they finally alighted; famous for porcelain, the native cattle, oak, communism and little else.

It was however beautiful. Wooded rolling countryside bisected by little streams and spotted with lakes. As with Zimbabwe, neither architecture nor culture were to the fore but nor were they so far away.

Perou was a small run -down farm in the north west of the region.

Hidden up a long track, one hundred and seven hectares of tired grass, ancient oak trees and rotting fences. The house, built of local stone, was joined to the barn. Both had seen better days.

The farm had been partially and entirely for sale many times without result, and the extended family who were its owners, were finally prevailed upon to act in unison.

It had the great merit of being cheap.

Mick had allowed himself cautious optimism on seeing the photographs and reading the description sent by Safer. Joy had already refused several not dissimilar properties on various grounds, but he could sense a growing resignation in her.

As it turned out, resignation was not needed. Weather and water won the day.

Glorious sunshine, a pretty lake behind the house and no man-made noise.

French bureaucracy was put in motion and a confirmatory visit on a dreich October day did not disappoint.

Quietly, they wound up their separate English lives and slipped away in the rush before Christmas.

Spender knew where they were headed, no one else.

If they stuck, there would be time for all that. If not, better private than public shame.

They came, they stuck, they began to prosper.

It was fun, an adventure, and in any case they had had no real choice.

It helped that there were no beguiling British siren voices telling them how brave they were, whilst secretly hoping for failure.

Spender made a regal tour of inspection, told them that they were mad and promptly checked in to a local hotel; it was very cold that winter.

The French were curious helpful and polite. Les Anglais were still considered exotic migrants in that part of the country. Not as common as they subsequently became.

It helped that they were farmers, which everyone around could understand, and a pretty girl is universal currency.

The first phase had two main aims.

Profitability, being the basis of survival. Fences were replaced to a more logical pattern. Pregnant ewes acquired and reseeding of pastures undertaken, despite the risk of a hot dry summer to follow.

Comfort, as Spender had observed, came lower on the list. The roof was sound so they were dry. Without dogs, bed would have been cold, the wiring was too ancient for electric blankets or kettles. They had a private water supply, so they were clean. Cheap wine for the soul and neither were fussy eaters.

The first lambing was a challenge. Mick had theoretical knowledge, Joy , practical. They muddled through. The attached barn meant nocturnal visits involved no distance and the grass came early that year.

Lambing percentages are probably the most lied about statistic in the world but it would have taken the creative genius of a Michaelangelo to flatter theirs.

However, if far from impressive, it was at least positive, and prices were French, not the miserable British version.

For this they had the French housewife, with her insistence on locally produced food, to thank.

Bills could be paid, improvements considered and a start made in local society.

Like most isolated rural communities, life revolved around crops, drinking, and killing things.

The cow was king and la chasse the queen.

Little competence or indeed participation was required to express a view on the former. The latter was taken much more seriously and proved to be the key that opened all doors.

Mick had a shotgun, an ancient Greener, and was given a dog by a neighbour who had too many .

A Munsterlander puppy, a sort of long tailed Spaniel with all that breed's enthusiasm, allied to an ability to point.

Joy had acquired a mare, a failed trotter, for the price of its flesh. It was young, fast, handsome and unspoiled by schooling. An undercoated canvas waiting for detail.

Just as a pointer is always welcome on a rough shoot, an elegant lady is appreciated on the hunting field, or in this case, forest.

The animals provided the entree, the humans followed as best, given their French grammar, they could.

It proved enough.

Abroad became less foreign and the present began to submerge the past.

The first child, a boy, came four years later to established and happy parents. While not unexpected, neither was he planned.

An insurance policy and focus for the future.

A daughter followed two years later at which point Joy

announced her retirement from the world of procreation.

Large families, she said, were for the rich which they were manifestly not.

They had one of each sex and, as she had cause to know, two's company, three's a crowd.

A sheep farm is an enveloping place for a child. Busy yet ordered, underlain with routine but spiced with the unexpected. There is always someone at home, there has to be. Against this stable background, Joy could begin to spread her wings.

Paint had been set aside, not forgotten.

From France, Italy was merely a short step away, and the art that she had seen as a girl she wish to emulate as an adult. Despite a heavy dose of self-pity, her husband agreed. A cage, he knew, does not make a happy home, and set against a lifetime, eight months is not that long.

It proved a sound investment. That Joy already had the talent was known, but technique must be learned.

Located near Florence, the studio was not one of those that cater to the English Finishing School market. All present expected to earn money from what they learned. All already had experience.

The various skills of Stucco, Fresco, Graffito and Scagliola were taught, practised and perfected. Joy had become an adept in a sparsely populated community.

Rarity has value and Joy could sell.

While the part of France in which they lived had little need of her new skills, this was not the case in the bigger cities.

Commissions to create or repair began to accumulate.

Work of this type has never been cheap and the discreet signs of affluence began to show at Perou.

Between jobs Joy was that best type of mother. Busy, fun and someone to be proud of.

Although they did not realise it at the time, the Bouleaus had one enormous advantage over their British peers.

French public education is effective.

An average child will emerge numerate, literate and

disciplined; something that requires an enormous financial outlay across The Channel.

A small farm cannot subsidise such expense, with or without sacrifice, condemning many children to the same toil and poverty as their parents.

Within a united Europe a French baccalaureate is as acceptable as A-levels, and both children opted for British universities; as foreign to them as France had once been to their parents.

Even their spoken English, as Spender frequently pointed out, sounded dated, although many said the same about him.

Chapter 27

Like a whore, the French port of St Malo has two faces.

One painted and pretty, the other strictly commercial.

Spender considered both with impatience as he waited for Mick to arrive at the ferry terminal.

Even the attractive side was a sham, he thought; the outside all granite and slate, underneath, 1950s concrete. A victim of the American air force during the last war.

It was a perfect late September morning, the sun slowly burning off a clammy mist, promising a hot and languid afternoon.

His boat had made good time, there had been few passengers that day and the French douane appeared to be on holiday.

At last, perhaps ten minutes late, a small green Peugeot pulled up in front of him and a smiling Mick climbed out to enjoy the complaints.

It had taken him a cockcrow start and some five hours of slow, quick, slow behind the inevitable lorries to get there. Despite the raised eyebrows opposite, he needed a stretch.

There are worse places than a harbour jetty and the presence of quayside cafes had a calming effect on his guest, as Mick had hoped they might. An early lunch later, they started on the return journey.

It was not a part of the country or route that Spender knew and he seemed to find little to favour along the way.

Rennes, it is true, is probably only beautiful to its denizens but Nantes is hardly Birmingham, as Spender proclaimed.

His curiosity sated, he lapsed into noisy sleep, surfacing occasionally to protest some song from Mick's collation.

They did not discuss the reason for his visit. This was not because it was exclusively Joy's affair; there were few secrets between the three. More it was the result of Spenders lunch, in particular the liquid portion. Siesta was vital, business could wait.

Nor was the subject broached that evening, the tone of Spender's emails and his urgent visit notwithstanding. There had been dogs to greet, changes to comment and more glasses to empty.

As they sat at the end of the garden by the lake watching the stars appear, the earlier unease Joy had felt evaporated. She had suspected all along that the fuss was less about her and more to do with Spender. It had happened before. But wine is an anaesthetic only if constantly administered. In the sober morning Joy knew that she was in trouble.

Spender was not easily worried, rattled, as Johnny Laidlaw would have put it. Nor was self- doubt a frequent ingredient in his internal recipe. Excitement sometimes, anger often. Yet this bright autumnal morning Joy could detect an unfamiliar unease behind the confident facade.

He had related the story of his meeting with Sir Merlin, suitably embellished to make his audience laugh. But all knew that the nightclub was dear to his heart, and only he knew how important to his complex finances.

His presence at Perou meant he took the threat seriously. Joy was the reason for that threat.

Spender had spoken to Johnny Laidlaw, had heard at first hand hand, the Scottish angle. Accounting discrepancies he understood, indeed was something of an expert.

He therefore much preferred the spotlight to be shone on others and did not appreciate the flickering beam sliding towards Montmorillon.

Johnny had mentioned the Dumfries rumour of missing money. True or false? If true, when, where and above all, how much?

Confession, they say, is good for the soul.

Allied to penance it can sweep away former sin. It is also strangely addictive.

Joy had not meant to say more than a bare minimum, merely to mention Matthew's final gift. However, once started, she found that she could not stop.

None of this, of course, was new to Mick but it had an electrifying effect on Spender. Anonymous bundles of cash with unexplained provenance were well within his competence and with Andrea's recent death the timing was clear.

There remained the puzzle of the two lawyers.

Apparently independent of one another, yet engaged on the same search.

But Joy had said all that she could, had no more secrets to unveil. The reason behind her desire for privacy was clearer than ever. It was also clear that others wanted to breach that wall.

It was in situations such as this that Spender showed himself at his splendid best.

She should not worry, he said. She had done nothing illegal. She should admit nothing. Curtail this silly urge to confession, contact no one else, take no further action whatever.

He would bring this whole ridiculous affair to a quick and final conclusion.

As it happened, he had to go to Scotland anyway. Now it would be sooner rather than later.

This was the angle from which to attack and he suspected it would illuminate the London end. It would certainly establish if there was a link between the two.

It was not necessary to add that he hoped also to switch Sir Merlin's jaundiced gaze from Montmorillon.

Everyone understood that.

One final thing. Did Joy still have the letters to Matthew from his mysterious girlfriend and could he see them?

It was very strange. Why would an employer give preciously hoarded and obviously secret love letters to his erstwhile cooks daughter?

Did he want them to be passed on?

To whom?

Was there are some hidden message for Joy? Or were they simply something from which he could not bear to be parted and for whom he had no other sympathetic recipient?

Joy had no idea but inclined to the latter viewpoint.

135

Spender thought differently, though why, he could not say.

He made copies of several of the letters. He also made Joy write an affidavit confirming that he was acting on her behalf with her full agreement.

It was signed in her maiden name and witnessed by her husband and later that evening the politely bewildered French dinner guest, Louis.

Chapter 28

If Sir Merlin paid more for his fishing, Joffrey could also cast a fly, perhaps with greater subtlety and certainly with extra patience. He was, therefore relieved rather than surprised to be contacted by Johnny Laidlaw.

He had suggested a meeting, this time in Edinburgh. He would be bringing, he said, an unnamed friend who might be able to help in locating Joy Turnbull.

The wording of the request was couched in words so far from Johnny's usual vocabulary that Joffrey had no trouble in guessing the 'friends' profession.

Spender had given Johnny's letter considerable thought and drafted it with care. He would have been pleased by Joffrey's appreciation.

His discussion with Johnny, some days earlier in London, had been similarly precise.

The reason for these orders had been largely lost on Johnny who saw only mystery and deliberate vagueness which he found irritating.

However, when he protested, Spender's reaction had been a contented smile and that usual wallpaper for lies,

'It's for your own protection, Johnny. What you don't know you can't reveal.'

What he did know, the little Spender divulged, was that Joy was well, happily married and living abroad; things that he had guessed long ago.

From Spenders interest in the detail of Petronella's gossip he surmised that they had some foundation in fact.

Names, places and dates he had supplied where he could. There was no reciprocity from Spender.

A letter had been drafted, fair copied in Johnny's own hand, signed and instructions given for its mailing from Scotland.

Spender, he said, would be a nice surprise for Joffrey.

After introductions had been made Johnny should retire.

Things, apparently, could be said between lawyers that laymen could not hear.

And what of the London end, the other legal chap, wondered Johnny? Again, Spender's reply was vague.

He had not confessed to Sir Merlin's threats, leaving Johnny puzzled by this untoward urgency.

Chapter 29

Two of the three participants in the Edinburgh meeting had an early start.

A radio alarm had burst into noisy life at the unusual hour of five thirty in the morning, not a part of the day with which Spender was on easy terms.

He stumbled out of bed in a somnolent daze and, in no particular order, attempted to shave, shower and make coffee.

It was too early for the hot water and coffee beans remained on the shopping list where they had been written some weeks previously.

Spender did not enjoy food shopping and although, by his own admission, a magnificent cook, the thought of washing up put him off. All in all, better to eat where preparation and reparation were carried out by someone else.

He did not need to pack, he was not planning on an overnight stay.

His briefcase, an eccentric Spanish affair of rough leather in the shape of a child's rucksack, held all that he would need and much that he did not.

He had no brief, will or certificates. Merely the copies of the love letters that Joy had shown him.

He would be flying blind and must trust his instruments, that keen faculty of his for sensing evasion and weakness honed by a thousand arguments.

A last look over the chaos of his drawing room, selection of suitable topcoat (Edinburgh was sure to be cold), ritual of alarm setting and he was away.

He gave the door its customary slam. The enmity with his Indian neighbour was mutual, and made a noisy descent of the staircase essential. If he couldn't sleep, he saw no reason why they should.

There was the usual pile of unopened mail in the lobby and, on a whim, he crammed some of it into his bag. It would give him something to read during his flight.

His beautiful car had collected its habitual overnight dusting of parking tickets and flyers which he calmly brushed away; the pleasure of Belgian number plates.

It was a short roll to the early-morning cafe and with a large espresso perched precariously on the dashboard he was off.

Often the theoretical merits of an early start fade with reality. This was not the case with Spender. He found compensation in speed. At that hour London was empty, any traffic heading in rather than out.

Everyone knows the urge to race where normally he must dawdle and everyone thinks that an engine benefits from a thorough blow through.

He slowed for the Watering Order of the Household Cavalry; that long file of equestrian leg stretching, but showed less consideration for the postmen and assorted delivery vans whose hour this usually was.

Leaving the horn blowing and looks of reluctant admiration in his wake, he fled the West End, alarmed the grey suited city robots shuffling to their desks in time for Asian closing and gained the open spaces of the M 11.

Here he slowed, lacking the camouflage of urban street and knowing the police propensity for pretty cars. In any event, he was making good time and preferred his present environment to that of Stansted, an airport that made him shudder.

Johnny Laidlaw held much the same opinion of early rising but was better acquainted with it. Lambing and calving are no respecters of nine to five. Often they can be trying but are, sadly, always essential for their role in funding that other, better, reason for quitting bed. Cub hunting.

It was the season, and despite it being a non-hunting day, the routine of a dawn start held sway.

Unlike Spender, Johnny was not alone in bed, nor was he awoken by an alarm. The first eastern tints were sufficient to rouse his companion, she as eager as anyone to be out and investigating what the night had left behind.

A long, languorous stretch followed by a vigorous shake was the signal to get up and Johnny obeyed.

140

He loved Nettie, his lurcher, very dearly.

They made their joint way down the back stairs to the kitchen, there to be greeted by a couple of stiff legged, greying Terriers.

A cup of tea made from the ever hot Aga kettle, gumboots pulled on over pyjama bottoms, an old coat, fags, matches and exit.

The normal ritual of communal pee, a sniffing of the air, glow of match to cigarette and off to the stable block.

As ever, all was fine.

Given the amount of time and money lavished there, it would have been odd if this was not the case. A fact ruefully acknowledged by Johnnie's many ex-girlfriends.

This routine over, he went back inside to dress, breakfast and telephone; actions which, by dint of long habit, he could perform simultaneously.

He would be away for much of the day and while shepherds and tractor men needed neither instruction nor supervision, it was as well, he thought, to confirm his continuing presence.

The girl groom was another matter but he would see her before he left.

A quick call to London revealed only an answering machine. He hoped that this meant Spender was on his way but, with him, one could never be sure. Both he and Spender had a long and justified mistrust of early-morning telephone calls.

And suddenly he was out of time.

Quick orders concerning horse exercise, the usual battle with Mrs Donoghue over the advisability of suit and tie in Edinburgh; rounding up Nettie, putting his current book into his father's old briefcase and they were off.

The A 68 was busy that morning, a combination of roadworks and lorries carrying components for the ever expanding wind farms; the new regional El Dorado.

Johnny had applied without success for the right to plant some of these propeller driven minting machines.

Several neighbours had them already and had virtually retired on the annual proceeds.

He had kept his application and subsequent refusal strictly private and was now a staunch opponent on moral, practical and aesthetic grounds.

This, he acknowledged to himself, was hypocrisy but a pack of foxhounds is an expensive toy and many others were guilty of the same double standards.

His destination was Edinburgh Airport. Spender claimed that he would need the ride into the city centre for last minute briefing and coordination. Johnny suspected that he merely wanted to avoid public transport.

He turned off the crowded road at St .Boswells to pursue the quieter and prettier A7. First following the river Tweed then veering north at Galashiels.

There were fewer lorries, the odd hardy commuter hurrying as was he, and the occasional tractor. Traffic hell was rejoined at the city ring road and continued all the way to the airport. Here the convoluted minds of urban planners and site engineers had turned an efficient medium-sized regional hub into an ever-growing snarl of one-way lanes and no- stop zones peopled by Polish builders and haggard passengers.

Among their number was Spender.

His look of intense irritation at being lumped with the common herd, forced like them to wait, gave Johnny a fillip. A fact signalled by the broad smile on his face as he illegally pulled over to pluck Spender to privacy.

This was authentic Spender.

One he recognised from the hard miles in the Blue Boat at Ely, where complaints had been many and ingenuous: from inadequate London restaurants to shooting days run with less than clockwork precision.

Safely gathered from the pavement, Spender gave vent to his frustration.

Johnny knew better than to intervene.

Indeed, all Spender's friends enjoyed the opening bars of a Spender symphony. A litany of the vast human venality and frailty aimed at the great man himself.

It would continue until the audience's enjoyment became too obvious when it petered out with weary resignation at the crass stupidity of the listener.

The remainder of the short journey passed in comfortable silence and the later search for a parking space.

The reason for their journey was briefly mentioned but all had been discussed before and Spender counted on Joffrey to move the matter forward.

As agreed, they would enter jointly and exit singly, Johnny first. When Spender was done they would reconvene in a bar of Johnny's choice to pool their findings.

Johnny had private doubts about Spenders inclination to 'pool', or to reveal future action.

Joffrey did not feature in their lunchtime plans.

They entered the offices of Don McCluskey and Younger WS after a brisk climb up Frederick Street. It was just before the appointed time of ten thirty.

The abstemious atmosphere and decor of austere disapproval had its familiar chastening effect on Johnny.

It did not seem to matter which Edinburgh legal firm he visited, he always felt himself summoned to the presence of some stern Victorian figure of authority. His old headmaster perhaps.

Such nuances were lost on Spender. His Chambers used the same sort of subliminal trick. They found it had a disciplining effect on self important clients.

They did not have to wait long; barely time to divest themselves of coats, before Joffrey emerged from his lair, scrubbed and sober, with a warm smile for Johnny and something harder for Spender.

Perfunctory introductions made, they seated themselves around the table in a sparsely furnished room. Coffee was called for and a clerk armed Joffrey with two folders, one fat the other almost empty.

It was Johnny who opened the bidding. He recounted, ostensibly for Spender's benefit, their earlier meeting and Joffrey's search for any information on Joy.

He explained that he had tried to contact her via email, but that since he had received no reply, he could not say whether or not he had been successful. He had therefore asked Mr Spender, an old and mutual friend, for help.

Mr Spender had had more luck as he would explain, but first, could Joffrey please furnish more detail on exactly what he wanted to know?

During their previous discussion he had intimated that his search was on behalf of a third party whose interest was benign.

He might, or might not, be aware that certain people in Dumfriesshire, whom he did not, for one moment believe, were casting scurrilous aspersions on Joy's character. And here, conscious of Spenders disapproving frown and firm pressure of hand on his arm, he ground to a red-faced halt.

'It had to be said. It's all rubbish founded on little more than jealousy and spite.'

This by way of explanation for his earlier outburst.

There followed that embarrassed silence where professionals commune telepathically on the wild and dangerous emotion of their clients.

To Johnny this empathy between his two companions was so obvious that guilt was about to prompt him to more self justification and apology.

He was saved by Joffrey and that humanity which comes with age.

'I am, as it happens, aware of certain gossip. Like you I discount it as the product of a small community that has little with which to occupy itself.

Nonetheless Mr Laidlaw, thank you for your frankness.

As to why I am trying to contact Miss Turnbull or whatever name she now owns to, that, I am afraid must remain between her and myself.

She may well choose to confide in you. I do not have that privilege. All I can say, reiterate; is that you and she may rest assured that I take no interest in local gossip. Quite the opposite in fact.'

Neither man missed the keening of interest in Spender. Joffrey understood immediately. It took Johnny a little longer but then he saw it too.

'Do you mean that it's happy rather than bad news?'

Joffrey inclined his head but answered with the question of his own.

144

'I would like, if I may, to retrace somewhat and start with you, Mr. Spender. If I have it right you are a friend, perhaps confidante of Miss. Turnbull. But why exactly are you here?'

In later years Johnny would remember this moment as if it had just happened. He had seen Spender in many guises but never, he realised, the professional one. It was as if, he would relate, Spender shrunk several inches in height, replacing them with a stubborn width.

His eyes became veiled, hooded lids, concentrating on some far point beyond the physical walls. His voice assumed an odd theoretical donnish delivery with very un-Spender like pauses, as if he was considering his own argument, (something which Johnny had never seen in Spender before). All this interspersed with sudden focus on the individual before him and a rapid stretching that restored him to his full height.

It was, realised a mesmerised Johnny, an act but with stagecraft good enough to have earned him a place in the Cambridge Footlights if the river had not beckoned first.

Spender did not reply to Joffrey's question. Instead he poked about in his peculiar rucksack, eventually retrieving an envelope which he passed across the table. It was the letter from Joy confirming his status.

Joffrey read it slowly, grunted and read it again. Finally, he moved his spectacles down his nose and gave Spender an appraising look. There were no words, just the offer of a business card from Spender.

'Like a bloody mime act.' As Johnny would later have it.

The card too was perused with care. Finally, the silent cinema ended. Johnny could only admire the sangfroid which Joffrey displayed.

'You will, I hope, understand and have no objection to me verifying this information?'

'Of course' said Spender, although his eyes said the opposite.

'I shall only be a minute or two' and Joffrey left the room to make his telephone call.

Johnny never found out to whom Joffrey had spoken.

Clerk or head of Chambers, the response had evidently been satisfactory. Given the twinkle in his eyes, perhaps even amusing.

In any event the horse trading could start and Johnny as the honest punter must leave.

He made his farewells and went.

He had been right, he thought, to bring his book. He sensed that they would be some time.

Spender spoke first, detailing the nature of his agreement with Joy and deliniating the limits of his brief. He used his boring voice.

'I have known Miss Turnbull since the early 1980s when I met her at University. She and her husband are close friends. You may consider this friendship prejudicial to unbiased advocacy but I shall do my best to remain impartial and you will, no doubt, let me know if you consider that I am straying.

Miss Turnbull lives abroad. Evidently she is married, this for the second time. The first union was a brief one, a mistake, happily without issue. The current marriage has lasted over twenty five years and there are two children, a boy and a girl both now over twenty years of age. Happily, from the legal angle, her husband is, and she remains, a British citizen.

For the moment and until I know the nature of your enquiry this is as far as I can go.'

This was not true. Joy had given Spender carte blanche but he was more parsimonious than she and preferred to reveal his hand card by card.

Joffrey too could advance slowly.

'I will return first to the affidavit. You say that this is written in your client's own hand, no doubt with your guidance as to wording?'

Spender nodded his assent.

'The two witnesses. They both seem to have francophone names although, unless my eyes deceive me, only one, the 'de' fellow, writes with a French hand?'

Sharper than he looks, thought Spender, irritated that he

had not noticed this detail. Yet it was true, the script was subtly different, not just individual style. More the result of a dirigist education system that requires conformity in all things, even those as small as writing.

Again Spender inclined his head.

'You are correct. 'De' is indeed French. A good friend to my client and sufficiently cosmopolitan to understand what he has signed. The other, despite the name, is British. No doubt, if asked, he would claim some ancient Norman ancestry.' And here Spender gave what was, Joffrey thought, his first genuine smile of the meeting.

'In my experience they often do.'

'This Mr. Bouleau. Could you please explain the nature of his relationship to your client? Is he another friend from foreign parts, or does he live in Britain?'

It was obvious where Joffrey's thrust was aimed although what had led him suspect, Spender could not say.

'Mr Bouleau is a long-standing friend of both my client and I. As with the Frenchman, he understands the nature of an affidavit and the consequences of his signature. I can vouch for the integrity of both men.'

Joffrey was not to be distracted so easily.

'So when you say long-standing, how long would that be? All the way back to university for example?'

And then, as if the idea suddenly occurred to him,

'You do, of course, realise that if he should turn out to be a relation of some sort, blood or otherwise, his right to bear witness would be compromised? Still, you have the other chap, the Frenchman. For my part, one will suffice. A Scottish court might find otherwise, something you should bear in mind.

Now, as to my interest in your client. It is quite simply stated. She is the beneficiary of an estate to which I am trustee.

She is not the sole beneficiary, there are two other principles and the usual scattering of small bequests.

The wording of my clients will is quite precise, leaving me little leeway and there are points which I must discuss with Miss. Turnbull before any distribution can be made.

147

In particular there are various discrepancies upon which, I hope, she can shine some light.

From my discussion with Mr Laidlaw you will have gathered that there are those who place an unkind interpretation on these discrepancies. Like he, I doubt this, but once rumour takes hold it can be hard to extinguish. Thus, I think, some urgency is signalled.'

'Good and bad news' thought Spender. It was heartening to perhaps think of some money coming Joy's way. She was long overdue a little gratuitous luck.

That which she had enjoyed had been very largely of her own making.

Discrepancies.

The strange suitcase of cash from Matthew fell into that category.

Should Joffrey mention this, his client would be unmasked. None other than Matthew. And if so even more curious. For what could have been his motive? Many sprang to mind but, in his experience, they usually revolved around fraud or sex.

He could not imagine Joy involved in either.

What also of the London angle?

Where did Sir Merlin fit in?

Indeed, was Joffrey even aware of this parallel quest?

He was tempted to go fishing; cast Matthew's gift on the water and see if he drew a bite. He was tempted to flavour this bait with London seasoning. Discover whether or not they were acting in concert.

Discretion however, prevailed. As much for his own safety as for that of Joy. He merely enquired in a mild tone,

'I wonder if you could detail, however briefly, these sins which gossip attribute to Miss Turnbull? These whispers, thanks to Mr Laidlaw, have reached as far as her but not the substance and one cannot defend oneself against unspecified charges.

If I am to be frank, I understand that their chief protagonist is a daughter of Miss Turnbull's deceased mothers erstwhile employer.

Laidlaw tells me that the lady is something of a specialist in this area.

Nonetheless, it makes me wonder why she cares and more generally whether there is some link between her and the estate which you represent?'

This was posed as a direct question, an eventuality for which Joffrey had prepared. He had not known in advance the extent to which Joy and Johnny communicated but, even if only infrequently, it was likely that Petronella's name would have occurred.

She was the chief mischief maker after all.

'Mr Spender I am going, like you, to be frank. I am sure I can trust your discretion and to advance we must have faith'.

A typical lawyer's touch thought Spender. Mix it up, announce openness when you plan to dissemble and substitute faith if facts are short.

He gave an encouraging smile. But Joffrey was true to his word.

'I will answer your second question first. The lady, principle in spreading this unpleasant gossip, is indeed a daughter of Mrs Turnbull's past employer.

She is also a co-beneficiary to the estate that I am endeavouring to wind up, as is her sister.

These two ladies are not yet fully aware of your client's interest. They merely know that the housekeeper's daughter is mentioned and speculate the most base reasons for her presence.

You will appreciate my problem. Mutual interest among those who do not consider themselves social equals.

You will therefore understand all the more readily why any discrepancy assumes a gravity out of all proportion to its actual size. This estate is, needless to say, the legacy of the two girls late father.

You, and I imagine your client too, will wonder as to the reason for her inclusion as a beneficiary. Whilst I know, it is not my secret to tell. There exists a letter of explanation from my late client to Miss Turnbull. It is very clear 'and with a sad smile, 'I know. I helped to draft it.'

Throughout this small history Spender had remained still.

149

He had listened to the story, trying to discern an underplayed or false note. He felt surprise but of degree not substance. The reason for spiteful rumour now obvious. However, all he said was, 'I see,' and proceeded to make some quick jottings in what Joffrey assumed was a private shorthand but was, in fact, his own atrocious writing.

'And now to your initial question. The sins, as you put it, of which your client is accused.

There are three, ah, discrepancies that need concern us.

They date to an inventory taken shortly before my client's death; the probate value of the estate and the actual situation thereafter.

None of them tally, one against the other, but they give a timetable of sorts for the unexplained loss of monies and chattels.

In chronological order, the first mystery is money. A withdrawal from my clients deposit account of a substantial sum. This alone was out of character. He was by nature a frugal man.

Neither his accountant nor I can reconcile these monies with any invoice or other acquisition. This of course does not, by itself, infer any sinister action. The money was his to do with as he wanted.

His widow and daughters thought otherwise and, sadly, consider your client the most likely explanation. Here I speculate, but if they are correct it is unfortunate that there is no written record.

A gift is a gift but in a household of suspicious women clarity is useful and there are also some tax implications.'

Spender, he saw, had started a list. This was item number one.

'Secondly, after the inventory but before probate, I have missing share certificates.

In ordinary circumstances this would present no problem.

The loss would be declared to the company registrar who would cancel the originals and issue duplicates.

Unfortunately these were bearer certificates, which as I am sure you are aware, come without title and devolve upon the physical holder.

They are, in essence, cash.

These particular certificates relate to an obscure Canadian mining company and date to the past century.

Even then they were a speculative investment, made as part of the drive to open up and develop the Imperial wilderness.

As far as I can tell they have been effectively valueless for over one hundred years. A time expired curiosity.'

Joffrey looked up.

'The Chinese have changed all that with their insatiable thirst for raw materials. The workings have been reopened: rare earth minerals I am told.

Apparently extremely valuable.

In any event, I have heard that there are several syndicates eager to buy the shares wherever they can find them.'

This information joined Spender's list under a second heading.

Joy had made no mention of share certificates when baring her soul to him and he felt sure that she would have.

He doubted whether either she or Mick were versed in such obscure objects. They would have asked for his opinion.

In any event, at the time of Matthew's surprise gift, they would have been worthless pieces of paper.

He hoped they had not been thrown away. Joy was more than capable of irrational but energetic spring cleaning.

Joffrey's final worry concerned, he said, a picture.

'A portrait to be exact. Attributed to Reynolds, although this may be merely family folklore.

A grand industrialist pictured with the trappings of his fortune, my client's ancestor. Too large to hang in the average house and too obvious to escape notice in the saleroom. It featured in both inventory and probate. It is not there now.

Here, I own that it can hardly have been taken by Miss Turnbull . Unless that is, she sidelines as a burglar, complete with team and removals van, as the oldest daughter seems to think.

I have a shrewd idea as to the whereabouts of this picture.

The first two items remain a mystery to me, even if another has already tried and convicted the perpetrator.'

Joffrey had finished even if Spender was still writing. It was clear that he expected a reply.

'All this is very interesting.' Spenders tone indicated a merely academic interest.

'I can see that these three discrepancies, as you call them, present you with an unpleasant dilemma.

Motive seems clear. Greed.

Mechanics, however present a problem, both in awareness of opportunity and wherewithal to seize the occasion.

As you mention, my client has had no dealings, much less physical contact, with your client's family for a very considerable time. Some twenty years.

She was the housekeeper's daughter, just a girl. Unlikely to have been privy to family business. Suspicion seems to be, in my opinion, more the result of avaricious speculation than logical reasoning.'

Here a change of tone. 'Nonetheless, perhaps I can help you with one item. First a question.

My client is also sought by another party, London based. They have contacted me in the same way that you contacted Mr Laidlaw.

Now this may be entirely coincidental but, given the retiring nature of my client and her, frankly, modest lifestyle it seems very odd.

Are you aware of this other interest and if so, does it concern the same subject? I apologise for being direct,'

Joffrey could discern no hint of an apology in the delivery, 'but you will understand my question.'

There was a calm silence.

Joffrey removed his spectacles, polished them with a neat white handkerchief, replaced them and turned to an earlier page in his file.

'Like you, I am suspicious of coincidence and I have some knowledge of what you ask. As it happens, this time it is coincidence but I am, indirectly, responsible for the questions being asked.

The link is your client. The objective much the same as mine but with a different source. I happened on this

152

information a little while back but have only recently made the connection.

There is nothing untoward in Sir Merlin Hayley's search.. Indeed, quite the opposite, but there is I believe a time constraint. It would, I think, be a mistake to delay too long.'

This time the surprise on Spenders face was evident.

Sir Merlins other source of information concerning Joy. He had been sure that it could not have been the Westminster connection alone.

A second completely separate legacy; both out of the blue.

Perhaps he should have married Joy himself.

'Sir Merlin Hayley; yes. As you may imagine we had met before our rather impromptu discussion of the other day.

He and his Chambers have a, how shall I put it, rather grand reputation in London legal circles. Can't think why.' This with a smile.

'I find his interest in Miss Turnbull, given her circumstances, puzzling. I don't think that she has been hiding her light under a bushel. She seemed genuinely surprised when I told her about London; she's not that good an actress.

This second matter, I take it, comes under English rather than Scottish jurisdiction?'

'That is my understanding. Certainly it has nothing to do with any client of mine, past or present.' This was not entirely true.

Spender continued. 'Well, I will put Sir Merlin to one side for the present and return to your three specific problems. Without prejudice to what you have told me; there may be no link whatsoever, I learned the other day of an odd event that took place many years previously.

It concerns the last occasion that my client and your client met; shortly before his death. As far as I'm aware she has told no one, beside her husband, of this event since.'

Spender began to relate Joy's story. He felt certain that this was where Joffrey's missing money had gone. He was equally sure that it had not been solicited by Joy. Begging for alms was not, nor ever had been, her style.

He outlined the sensitive, almost furtive, nature of her

153

visit. He emphasised the hasty way the gift had been made. Matthew's emphasis on discretion, even concealment.

Joffrey, he noticed, was nodding. The poisonous atmosphere of Gladdies at that time was something he could well picture. He had seen it for himself. He had summoned Joy to Matthew's bedside.

Spender continued. The gift, a wooden box, was not explained, he said. It's contents not mentioned. Just that Joy had known by the look on his face that they were precious to Matthew. It was, she had said, rather like being handed something sacred. Something between he and she alone. Something, she felt instinctively, that was very private to him; not shared with the rest of his family.

Here Joffrey interrupted with, what was to Spender, a very peculiar look upon his face.

'You are absolutely certain that my client said nothing of the contents of this box?' The question seemed vital.

'Yes I am certain. Nothing was said. My client was adamant about that point. Only that it was their secret.

Above all she wishes now, given the contents, that she had had a chance to ask questions. He died so quickly, perhaps before she had even opened it, I do not know.

She was in London, he in Scotland and she tells me that no telephone call in that farmhouse was ever really private.'

This Joffrey could well believe.

'I'm sorry. Please go on.'

Spender continued the story.

How Joy had hidden the box in her car, said her farewells and fled.

Had cried her way back to London.

Tears for a man she loved. Loved as if he had been her father.

Tears for that rare thing, a truly good man dying alone among hard faced strangers even if they were his own wife and daughter.

And finally, tears because she sensed that this had been a last meeting, that she would never see him again.

Joffrey seemed entranced, even a little moist around the eyes. Or perhaps it was only Spender's imagination.

It had been a shock, a real shock, Spender said, when she finally summoned up the courage to open the box. She had had no idea what to expect. Certainly not money. Perhaps a memento of Gladdies that had meaning for her. A trinket that the family might not miss but, nonetheless, begrudge the giving of.

Instead there had been bank notes. Lots of them. This, she knew, they would miss. She was astonished.

There had also been letters, he said. Carefully folded letters. By their patina, often re-read, then folded again and tied together in chronological order. All from the same woman, pre- dating the marriage and, obviously, very much loved.

'There is also one, just one, with a more recent date. The same lady. She had apparently heard your client speaking on the wireless; something to do with hunting.

Why she decided to write then; whether she received a reply; indeed who she is or was, is a mystery to my client. Why was she given these letters? The money she can understand, the letters not.'

Again, Joffrey seemed in the grip of some sad emotion, a faraway look in his eyes. He had shown no obvious satisfaction at the mention of the money. No hint that one item on his ledger of discrepancies could be crossed off. The letters had his full attention.

'He knows what they are,' thought Spender. 'Will he confess?'

Finally Joffrey roused himself.

'These letters you say, apart from one, all date to the period before my client's marriage?'

'That's right. I did not read them all but Miss Turnbull was specific about the fact and almost haunted that he had given them to her. I told her that he obviously could not bring himself to get rid of them; that no wife likes to be reminded of earlier loves. Especially a love so studiously hoarded.

She plans, I think, to burn them and scatter the ashes in her garden. In lieu of him, so to speak.'

This last statement jerked Joffrey to a sudden and

surprising animation; like a lizard that has lain motionless until it darts at a fly.

'No! Under no circumstances must she do that. Please tell me that she has not already done so. Tell her not to, tell her today. Those letters may prove to be vital. I am not exaggerating.'

'As it happens, I also wondered if they had a significance greater than the immediately obvious. After all, it is a strange thing to do. Why give a bundle of ancient love letters to your housekeeper's daughter, family secrets or not? I told her to hold onto them for the meantime. I also took the precaution of making copies of a few, including the last one. I have them here if they would interest you, but first the money that you mentioned. It appears to tally with your figures?'

He still was not interested.

'Yes. Yes the money. It would seem that that's that accounted for. I can see why it was done as it was. Making a gift in that fashion is certainly no crime. It is a pity that he didn't record it somewhere, but that was typical of him.

The family will never believe that she didn't wheedle it out of him in some underhand way. Not until the final division that is.'

And here Joffrey brightened, 'Still, there's no rush to tell them, is there?'

And with that enigmatic pronouncement he returned to the subject dearer to his heart.

'I do not mean to condescend when I congratulate you on your perception concerning those letters. If they are from whom I think, my client kept them initially from emotion, latterly for a good reason. It was no accident that he gave them to Miss Turnbull. May I see them please?'

Spender had taken copies of six from the bundle of over thirty. They had all seemed much the same. Intimate, chatty and passionate. Answers to questions that he could only guess at. A longing diary of separation. In short, pretty standard fare between any girl and her faraway boyfriend. He had, in his time, received plenty.

Joffrey, however, seemed spellbound; reading each letter

156

with studied care as if to decipher some hidden meaning.

Spender left him to it while he, in turn, tried to unravel a plausible connection between the author of the letters and Joy.

Joffrey had hinted that there was such a link. It was not obvious to Spender and he was sure that Joy had no inkling. The best he could come up with was some modern day fairy godmother.

This reminded him of nursery teas which led in turn to food and lunch; something, he realised, that was becoming overdue. Breakfast had been unsatisfactory. And long ago.

His reverie was broken by Joffrey, a more measured Joffrey than hitherto. A sterner tone but not without kindness. A warning.

'I never met the author of these letters but yet I feel that I know her. Despite her physical absence she was never far from my client's thoughts.

He had, you may say, a constant reminder.

I cannot go further at present. Suffice it to say, they are important. Proof if you will.

Tell Miss Turnbull to keep them safe. They are now, and in the future will be even more, important to her.. You will find Sir Merlin also interested.

I urge you to see him soon. Show him the copies, especially the last, keep the originals.

I should not really say this, but between ourselves, he may find such proof, how shall I put it? Awkward.'

There was an equally awkward silence although Spender was certainly not averse to a little Sir Merlin baiting if the opportunity should come his way.

'In the meantime please pass my regards to Miss Turnbull . I hope that I have convinced you that she has nothing to fear and indeed much to gain by meeting me. Her private affairs are no concern of mine and her whereabouts need not be disclosed.

If I may impose, I suggest that you meet with Sir Merlin before any further contact with me and perhaps even your client. I cannot forecast his reaction to these letters, but they should convince him of your client's identity. He can be a little, ah, obstreperous.

After that I think a further meeting between us, perhaps including Miss Turnbull, would be useful.

Please let me know how you get on and do not hesitate to contact me if I can be of any help.'

So the first contact, as Spender later thought of it, ended. It had been satisfactory, with the promise of future revelation.

It seemed that Joy's life was about to be turned over, hopefully for the better.

He had already decided to play it dull with Johnny. Good gossip is hard to keep to yourself. Not that Johnny would, but when refreshed his loyalty to Joy might verge to indiscretion. Better not to take that chance.

Chapter 30

A lawyer will tell you that there are three main categories of guilty party. The first is in denial. Unable or unwilling to face the consequences of his action. He, or she, prays that the truth will remain forever buried.

The second displays the inverse of these characteristics. An urge to confession, a shriving of the soul so as to be reborn pure. He hopes, naturally, that any penalty will not be too onerous, perhaps even avoided entirely. But if penance there must be, he is ready to pay.

The third doesn't give a damn.

Joy belonged to the second category. She had told Spender of her sin and he had visited the temple to receive judgement. She had placed herself in his hands, had faith in his advocacy. As her husband had dryly observed, this was not surrender, Spender could and would argue with God. Out of principle and for his own high standards, if for no other reason.

Nonetheless, the wait for his report was trying. Not knowing what to expect, but fearing the worst every night in her dreams. It was hardly surprising that this time Spender received a prompt reply to this email.

He had stated the bald facts gleaned from his time with Joffrey. If the money had been a source of worry, it need be no longer. That was the official view. The case was closed.

It might continue to be the inspiration for Petronella's rant. It was not pleasant, but sticks and stones etc.

As to the letters, the mist was lifting but the view still not clear. For reasons that he would not divulge, Joffrey considered them vital.

He, Spender, would not speculate why, but it seemed that they had relevance to the London enquiry. This he would like to tackle next. Could he go ahead?

Joy read and digested the news with relief. She was also puzzled. They had all assumed that the Scottish and the

London searches were linked. Part of the same enquiry. Spender had merely said that they might be relevant. He was being mysterious.

She began the trial by telephone that was the fate of all who attempted to ring him.

Eventually they connected. Spender was in upbeat mood, more inclined to talk of his latest idea, the global franchise of the Montmorillon brand, than discuss her mundane affairs. He waved away her questions. France was a duck pond, he said. Think big. Invest while the recession lasts and bargains abound.

'That wonderful contagious Spender largesse' Joy cheerfully thought. 'Only matched by the depth of victimised outrage when events go against him.'

She had often been witness to the gestation of such world beating schemes, normally quickly superseded by even better projects or abandoned after a fatal collision with reality.

It was impossible not to enjoy a Spender diatribe, high or low. When he finally relented she had forgotten her question but laughingly said, 'I'd love to join this sure fire gravy train but, sadly, the French duck pond is fresh out of funds; that is, unless you want to lend.'

Spender caught himself. He had almost said that he suspected all that was about to change. An instinctive self-preservation held him back. Those who raise expectations which prove unfounded must live with the consequences. Toothpaste is not easy to put back in the tube.

Instead, he calmed, invoking Joys immediate suspicion.

'Now, I don't think so thank you. It's not you Joy, you understand. But my shareholders would never approve a loan to that shifty little man you married. Never trust a rebadged colonial.

Back to business. That Scottish solicitor, Joffrey. Dusty old boy but decent enough. Parochial, needless to say. He's head trustee of Matthew's estate and he needs your presence before it can be wound up.

Now don't get excited and for heaven's sake don't tell the stumpy dwarf but you are a beneficiary. God knows why.

160

You will know better than me what Gladdies is worth, but I don't suppose the going rate for fresh air and rocks has changed much since your day.

In any event you've already had your secret suitcase, about which Joffrey was supremely unconcerned, so I wouldn't expect too much. You'll have to see him to learn more.

I'll come and hold your hand if you like and then, if I'm wrong and you turn into Rockefeller, I'll mug you on the way out.'

Joy was about to interrupt but Spender was in full flow.

'Now, the London end. Joffrey has a hand there also, but won't say why. Nonetheless, a betting man would lay odds on a tie- in with Matthew somewhere down the line. I'm speculating, you understand. With your permission, I would like to go and see him. The sooner the better, given what he had to say about my nightclub, the old goat.

Of course, I'll deal with your stuff at the same time.'

'Hurrah' thought Joy. 'At least I'm not totally forgotten in the Montmorillon induced miasma', but she didn't say so. It would only have made him cross.

'Joffrey also wants me to show Sir Merlin the letters. That all right? No mention of your suitcases other contents, needless to say. I think the cash is Joffrey's affair alone.'

Thus he skilfully deflected Joy's forming question about Sir Merlin's motives. He need only mention the guilty gold to mask the scent of the rest. He certainly did not want to raise the prospect of another legacy. It might only be a product of his own imagination spawned by the obscure language of an old Edinburgh solicitor. Wait and see.

Joy's consent gained, Spender started to plan his assault on Sir Merlin. He was forewarned; had seen how quickly the man went for his knife. He too would come armed.

Spender had never been taken by the military life. The long gap between Lieutenant and General did not appeal. Nonetheless, any soldier would have recognised his mental process.

First the aim. This, as far as he was concerned, was to

161

avoid the roving eye of the Inland Revenue falling on him in general and Montmorillon in particular.

The business with Joy fell under the heading 'exploitation'. Something secondary. Only to be attempted once the main aim was achieved.

Enemy.

Clearly Sir Merlin. He would need to hone his intelligence here. How?

Friends. A nightclub owner and bachelor about town has many friends. He made a note of those who might be useful. Finally he considered the courses open to him and his ultimate route.

He began by securing his base. Lawyers are like fish in the sea. There are an infinite variety but, generally, the bigger prey on the smaller.

He chose the great white shark of tax experts, by happy chance a rowing man. It was expensive but tranquillity for nightclub owners does not come cheap.

He left poorer but reassured. His natural instinct for complication had left the nightclub inviolate to all save an accounting Einstein. The great white shark doubted that such a man had yet been born.

Next on his list was Sir Merlin. The expert had raised eyebrows at the mention of this name, which suggested promise. The old far eastern trading houses have many buried skeletons but Spender was warned against the dissent and dither of financial archaeologists. It cost.

He would go the tabloid route. Concentrate on flesh.

Chapter 31

Archie Lloyd was surprised but delighted to receive an invitation from Spender for a night on the town. He loved nightclubs. His wife did not.

Archie was a tall slim man with a keen sense of fun concealed behind a shy and dutiful front. The latest holder of a grand and ancient title, he was the happy beneficiary of nearly one thousand years of West Country breeding. He owned considerably more than that in acres.

His wife had known Johnny Laidlaw at Cambridge, thereby met Spender and so it went.

Life, as Spender dispassionately observed, is small at the top.

He had often graced the Lloyd domain, gun in hand, so Archie found nothing untoward in the offer of a return match to the Big Smoke.

Dinner was taken in Spender's club. Black tie, with a noisy crowd of colleagues to act as unwitting camouflage. By and by, Spender engineered the conversation to politics and its strange practitioners. Like most normal men, Archie did not know many, but the one he did, Sir Merlin, gave him the chance to regale his audience.

There could be no harm, he thought, the man was retired from Parliament. He was a pompous, finicky tenant and the present company was discreet. No kiss and tell here.

Amidst the fug of brandy and bonhomie he started.

'The name Hayley, Merlin Hayley, sorry; Sir Merlin Hayley ring any bells? My erstwhile MP, still my tenant.

The genius who turned a rock solid Tory constituency into a Liberal creche in a single term?'

The response was immediate. These were the up and coming men. Making their way as bankers, brokers and lawyers. The cream of their age group. The next generation of the establishment. Ears to the ground, certainly they had heard of him. Many had their own Hayley anecdotes but meantime they cheered,

'Go on!'

'Funny man. Hayley money of course. China and all that.'

'Opium!' They chanted, confusing the club waiter who was hovering nervously nearby.

'One minute Merlin we called him. That's all the time he ever gave us. Fussy tweed suit, club tie surgically attached, limp-ish handshake and a minute's worth of platitudes.

Mousey wife, regulation labrador, spotless Range Rover, expensive daughters, so far so dull. But then', and he primed his public with a studied pause and wide smile,

'Madame Whiplash'.

He had them hooked. 'Go on! Go on!'

'It was a beat keeper who saw it. Told me. Used to hypocrisy, but not from such a staunch defender of family values. Especially one who constantly complained about pheasants digging up his dahlias. Idiot. Can't tell feather from fur.' And then he shouted 'Rabbit forward!' Sufficiently loud to turn several heads and bring the waiter scurrying.

'Breaking dawn, the milkman's hour, checking his traps and greeting Charlie on his way home.

Cammo jacket, quiet behind the hedge.

Suddenly an exotic species steps out of the Hayley house. Certainly didn't feature on any normal Game Card.

Melanistic, he said, but not all wings and sinew, instead plump and fluffed up.

MP gives furtive glance, push- off kiss and away she goes. VW golf, very discreet.

Daughters friend? Auntie Lettice? My man doesn't think so.

Next weekend, same time, same plumage. Weekend after? Same time, different bird.

Within a couple of months he'd worked his way down to the 'Various' column. A man happy in his job. And that's just my keeper!'

Spender joined in the general laughter with an ear open to the competing Hayley stories that followed.

They were the usual bumph that follows any public figure. Old hat innuendo from the gossip columns, spiced with occasional personal detail resulting from a Hayley snub. Nothing useful.

He made a mental note to seek out the observant beat keeper when he was next down. Charm, a handsome tip and easy manner often unstuck even the most reticent retainers tongue.

He now had ammunition should he need it.

The menace of Sir Merlin was on the wane.

The remainder of the evening passed, while not quietly, with no incident of note. The nightclub had been crowded, the two Princes were rumoured to be in town. The club was known as one of their favourite haunts and the usual crowd of celebrity seekers had turned up. So had the paparazzi, only to be disappointed.

Finding the pickings slim, they had turned their lenses on the dinner jacketed toffs who emerged shortly after two in the morning.

It was hardly a scoop, but the news was slow that day. Thus it was that a photograph appeared in the society column of the evening paper.

'Peer of the realm enjoys night out 'read the caption which accompanied a featherweight space filling paragraph.

It passed unremarked save in two households.

Archie's wife, in London for the shopping not the clubbing, saw it and said that he and Spender looked drunk. She was right about the former but not the latter.

Sir Merlin spotted it also, but through less frivolous eyes. It could, conceivably, be innocent coincidence. It was hardly unknown for the aristocracy to enjoy nocturnal high jinks but that wretched upstart Spender had mentioned Lloyd by name, and here they were, hugger mugger. It was a thoughtful Baronet who went to bed that night.

The upshot was a telephone call to Spender's Chambers the next morning. Sir Merlin was at his unctuous best. He apologised for the nuisance, but wondered if Spender had made any headway in the matter previously discussed. His clerk was being tiresome, he said.

Recognising this smooth charm for the alarm signal that it in fact was, Spender prevaricated.

Yes, he replied. He had a lead which he thought promising. He would know for sure in, say, a fortnight. Could they provisionally fix a rendezvous then?

Sir Merlin could and a date was duly entered in two diaries.

But while Sir Merlin could only wait with uneasy impatience for the arbitrary day Spender had a timetable and clear objective.

Archie Lloyd had invited him for a day on the partridges.

Chapter 32

The countryside was not looking its best that weekend. It had been a wild end to September, all wind and rain. Judging by the rattling of the windows, October was starting in the same vein.

He had driven down the night before, following the usual snake of homeward bound commuters and four wheel drive weekly boarder mothers.

Finally, the traffic had thinned and then died altogether. North Devon remained, thank God, resolutely rural.

The evening had been liquid and jolly, the Lloyds knew how to put together a good house party. Johnny Laidlaw was there. Given the frequency with which he appeared all over the country, Spender wondered how he ever found time to hunt, much less farm.

They had been given a room to share and Johnny was already awake, he saw, leafing with incredulity through the selection of new age tomes that graced their bedside table. They came as no surprise to Spender. Maggie Lloyd had long been a seeker of alternative truth in the way only the very rich or truly eccentric are.

Happily, it did not stop her doing the traditional things comfortingly well.

Breakfast was certainly traditional. It was followed by the traditional rush and muddle finding hats, boots, coats, guns and cartridge bags.

Spender avoided this as best he could in splendid isolation on an upstairs loo. He doubted he would see another until the evening and outdoor ablutions were not to his taste.

Eventually they crammed into a tractor pulled trailer and were off to the morning's playground. It was, as always, superb. The steep little valleys with rocky little streams. The carefully sited woods, planted by generations of Lloyds, now long dead. The thick game crops put in by Archie and his keepers that year. They all yielded their harvest.

This was, thought Spender, as far from the brash commercial days, so beloved by the corporate entertainers, as it was possible to get.

No noise, save the tap- tapping of sticks from the unseen beating line. No clouds of low, tame poultry. No newly be-tweeded wideboys wildly firing at anything with their heavily engraved best London guns. Just a steady trickle of birds, fast, high and wild. He only wished that he could hit more of them. A sentiment, unbeknown to him, shared by his fellow guns all along the line.

It was a long drive followed by a pause for bullshot and sausages. Those guests who had bought their dogs joined the thorough team of picker- uppers. Johnny's lurcher had been excused the day. The remainder swapped lies and compliments on the standard of shooting. Spender sought out the young beat keeper who had so fortuitously stumbled upon Sir Merlin's hobby.

He was a fit looking man, smartly dressed in the estate tweed, busily engaged in pairing and hanging birds on the game cart.

Spender emptied his pockets of spent cartridge cases into the bucket provided, noting ruefully how many there were.

'You've had a good stand, Sir. In the hot seat were you?'Came the smiling comment.

'Certainly was, although I'm afraid I haven't troubled the pickers up much. Fantastic birds, much too good for me. How do you do; Saville Spender.'He offered his hand.

'Ed Trevenick, I'm the keeper for this bit. Glad you're enjoying yourself.'

With the break between drives continuing, Spender reached for his cigars, offered one which was politely refused and started on the usual small talk that passes between all visiting guns and those who supply their sport. They spoke of weather, disease, predators and poachers.

Seamlessly Spender moved the conversation to the local community and, as if by accident, to the sensitive subject of weekend and holiday home owners.

'Drive up the prices, I imagine?'

'Certainly do. An agricultural wage doesn't get you far down here. But we are lucky. House comes with the job and the estate hardly ever sells. Mainly long term lets, that way we know who we are dealing with.'

Many make the pilgrimage from the grimy streets of London? It's a long way for a weekend.'

'More than you'd think. They have their private little bolt holes away from the crowd. Give us plenty of entertainment, some of them. Don't seem to realise that a gamekeepers about all hours. Take that one there for example,' pointing to a pretty cottage tucked into the next valley,

'Ageing big cheese. Wife and kids in town. Something else down here. Sunday mornings, five thirty, you could set your clock by him, although with the birds out of the pens now I'm not so often about. Topping up the feeders isn't nearly as much fun without the floorshow.'

They changed topics to Exeter's prospects for the coming rugby season and then they were off again. A walk to the next stand. But Spender was satisfied. His planned detour for the next morning should go unobserved.

The day had been enormous fun. Lunch, old-fashioned and hearty, tea more of the same. Both the Lloyds had tried to make Spender changed his plans for an early departure the next day, but knew the probable futility of such entreaties. When his mind was made up he was as stubborn as a child.

Neither believed his excuse of work; a big case starting on Monday. They suspected a girl, which was, in fact, the truth but not in the way they imagined. If he really had to leave at the un-earthly hour of four forty five, then so be it.

He signed the visitors book that night and took himself to bed.

Johnny, however, was having none of it. He had never known Spender to work on a Sunday. Not for love. Not for money. Not even for his disastrously under researched Cambridge Finals.

He tackled him head on and Spender's resolve began to wilt.

He was, he admitted to himself, nervous about what he

planned to do. An unusual sensation and not one that he was enjoying.

Conceal himself near Sir Merlin's cottage at the appointed hour, take photographs if it was not too dark and at the very least, make a note of license plate numbers.

The plan had seemed simple back in London. A straightforward thing. Now he had nagging doubts.

He had done no prior reconnaissance of the site. Could he get in and out unobserved? What if Sir Merlin saw and recognised him?. He wasn't even very good with cameras , especially when they were attached to a telephoto lens. He had heard the expression, 'a burden shared is a burden halved': he decided to put it to the test. He told Johnny.

The reaction was not what he expected. It took Johnny a full minute to stop laughing. No one likes to be greeted with hilarity on divulging a dark and dangerous secret and Spender was no exception.

Seeing the cold stare, Johnny quietened and attempted to calm Nettie the lurcher who had assumed that this was a game.

He asked for the story again from the beginning and listened carefully, seeing the plan with a countryman's eye, not the slightly dramatic spy story that Spender told.

He was tempted to ask the obvious question, 'Why?'But doubted the truth of any answer . In the end he did not have to bother. Spender told him without prompting, although his focus was mainly Joy and Montmorillon just an appendix.

Subconsciously or otherwise, Spender had made a good decision. Johnny was the right man in the right place. He had long experience of furtive pre-dawn escapes from illicit bedrooms and a natural eye for cover, born of teenage poaching and present day fox hunting. He was also a good actor, could play yob or snob with equal flair, and his usual attire covered both eventualities.

Likewise the lurcher. Depending on the prejudice of the beholder it was either gypsies cur or gentleman's gazehound. Sir Merlin would likely take the former view. Thus they,or rather Johnny, made their plan.

They would go together. Spender drop him back

afterwards. If they were seen by the Lloyds, not probable he thought, he would simply say that Spender had woken him by crashing about and the dog needed a pee.

They would get there early, leave the car out of sight, walk in quietly and he, Johnny, would select what he called the 'Hide'. He would then retire to a point where, although invisible, he could see both Spender and the cottage. He would wait, staying still until he saw the lady leave. Then he and Nettie would appear as if on nefarious business.

This, he said, would get their attention, deflect their gaze from Spender's direction and give time for photographs. Sir Merlin would not feel threatened. Poachers don't tell self incriminating tales.

It all sounded unnecessarily complicated to Spender and he made Johnny promise to remain concealed unless it seemed likely that he would be compromised. Johnny agreed

with reluctance. It was obvious that he was keen to have his walk on part. In any event, it was a plan and it had a safety exit.

Their joint enterprise started well. They rose early, gave themselves a cup of coffee and left without disturbing the sleeping household.

Spender reversed his car into a muddy field entrance around a bend and some quarter of a mile distant from their target. They crept in and once Johnny had sited Spender, hidden behind a hedge opposite Sir Merlin's driveway, he continued up the hill to watch.

There were two vehicles parked at the front of the cottage so they were hopeful that their quarry was at home.

Having fiddled with his camera and been stung by nettles in various places Spender settled, uncomfortably, to his vigil. He did not have long to wait.

First came a light upstairs and mime show of shadowy silhouettes seen through drawn curtains.

This was then extinguished in favour of a hall lamp and, despite the wind, voices; one male, one female.

They had different accents but both sounded cross.

Then action. It all happened very fast and it was only later that Spender managed to place events in their proper sequence.

The opening scene. An abrupt and unannounced push of the front door to reveal Sir Merlin, resplendent in slippers and Paisley dressing gown, remonstrating with a yellow track suited girl, young enough to have been Spender's daughter.

It was obvious that the opportunity for photography would be short. The girl was already striding towards the smaller car.

He raised his camera, the focus already set, and fired.

The resulting exposure was clear, the next few seconds anything but. In the nanosecond it took to depress the shutter, the robotic brain of the camera, quite rightly, judged the ambient light level too feeble for what it was being asked to do.

Its powerful flash exploded the dark, knocking a startled Spender backward into the plough and freezing the equally stunned couple into digital rigidity.

Three things then happened at once. Spender bolted, fear lending wings to his feet despite the wet clay that clung in clods to his shoes.

Two doors slammed, Sir Merlin going to ground. The girl gunning her engine with an expensive grinding of gears and spinning of gravel.

Between the two came Johnny at the trot, grinning from ear to ear, Nettie bouncing alongside.

Sadly for Johnny, but perhaps fortunately, his audience was small. A fleeting glimpse in a fast receding rear view mirror. A fuzzy impression from a sitting room window and a long incredulous stare from the opposite hillside.

They met breathlessly back at the car.

'Fucking cheap Korean piece of shit' was Spender's only comment. The workman blaming his tools.

Johnny saw it differently.

'Unbelievable old cock. Unbelievable. Bloody nearly shat myself laughing. Should have seen their faces. Heart attacks all round. Probably better call an ambulance for the old boy. His pacemaker will have gone critical.'

And then looking at Spender, 'what happened to you?

Been celebrating with a mud bath? Got the number plate by the way; thought you might be busy.'

With a happy kiss he popped Nettie into the car and they pulled out of the gateway onto the lane, driving fast but lightless to the T-junction at the bottom.

To their joint horror there was a Land Rover blocking their exit.

'Good morning Sirs. Hope the piccy comes out all right. Oh, please watch the dog, lots of birds about. Best be getting on, lots to do.' And then with a large smile,

'Top of the morning to you both' and Ed Trevenick went on his steady way.

Funny friends his Lordship has, he thought. Poor shots but nice enough chaps and, the big one especially, good tippers.

Chapter 33

'Love Cheat Q C's Bonking Bungalow Hideaway.'

It had, praise the Lord, not happened. Perhaps it was only a figment of Sir Merlin's guilty imagination.

He had made an early, almost manic, review of the daily papers, especially those titles normally read by his wife and daughters, since that fateful Sunday.

Perhaps it had not been a tabloid crusader. Certainly there had been that poacher chap and his dog running like hell, but the flash had been more bulb than crowscarer and he could not recall any bang.

After some reflection he had reported the incident to the local gamekeeper in what he assumed to be a worthy but helpful tone. The insolent fellow had simply responded, 'Very likely,' and then admonished him to take more care when driving. Road crossing pheasants indeed!

Better lie low, he thought. Take a sexual sabbatical for two or three months. If nothing had happened by then, he was probably in the clear. And still there was that arrogant young barrister waiting in connection with the Playfair trust. He had, it seemed, something to report. Some information concerning that shadowy beneficiary.

It would take a great deal to convince him of this girl's bona fides. A blood group test, he thought with satisfaction. The prospect of a needle often set the goats running even before they mixed with the sheep.

Then there was the question of her background.

The manners of the hill farm remained just those, however blue the blood that filled the body.

No. Mr Spender would not find Sir Merlin Hayley an easy ride.

First, proof that this girl was who she purported to be.

Second, if that threshold was crossed, her ability and suitability to manage any legacy. He would be failing in his duty as trustee if he did not satisfy himself on this point.

Sir Merlin could, as his Devon ladies knew, be hard to satisfy.

'What an extraordinarily vulgar room' thought Spender has he was finally ushered in.

'The half hour wait, heavy club- land furniture and Wall of Fame. The man must be terminally insecure.'

It was true that while the decor might suggest gravitas to mid Europeans or Americans, it had quite the opposite effect on members of Sir Merlin's own milieu..

Boasting has never been considered quite the thing in British society. Better left to foreigners or politicians.

A minion was floating deferentially behind Sir Merlin and was introduced in an offhand way as Justin.

'Either here as stuffing, or as he's the worker bee'was Spender's judgement. Time would quickly tell.

The minion, he noted, was wearing a Hawk's Club tie, marking him as a sometime Cambridge Blue.

'Own one of those myself,' he said indicating his own and flapping the end,

'Rowing. What's yours?'

The reply of 'table tennis' did little to reassure.

Sufficiently annoyed by the whole atmosphere, Spender decided on the direct approach. Originally he had been tempted, with a sense of lingering unease over his photographic expedition, to start by probing. Sir Merlin's theatre had restored his natural swagger.

'At our last meeting you told me I knew a lady called Miss Joy Turnbull. You stated I had met her at Cambridge and you intimated I might know her present whereabouts. You wanted to contact her. You did not tell me why.

I replied that I would make enquiries.

My enquiries have borne fruit.

I have managed to find the lady in question and been in contact with her. She has seen fit to let me act for her.'

Here he produced the same letter that he had shown to Joffrey.

'She would like to know why you want to see her before proceeding further.'

Sir Merlin took his time over the affidavit. He passed it to Justin, then reclaimed it for further scrutiny. Spenders question, however, hung between them; a door that must be opened before further progress could be made.

Like any good barrister Sir Merlin took refuge in prevarication.

'This letter. I have only your word that it is what it purports to be.'

'That, I'm afraid, Sir Merlin, is all that you're going to get.'

Spender was brutal. He had always enjoyed squashing popinjays.

Sir Merlin, used to the deference usually shown him, was unprepared for this assault. With a series of blustery sighs he stretched himself and then seemed to deflate.

'Toad of Toad Hall' thought Spender, watching an ephemeral smile cross the neutral face of Justin.

'Miss Turnbull, quite reasonably in my opinion, wants to know why she is summoned before responding to the bell. I imagine you would have the same reaction.'

And then, for sheer pleasure, 'Miss Turnbull, for better or worse, has not been subject to Pavlovian conditioning.'

This was simply rude and Spender knew it. He was not a bully but Sir Merlin had threatened him. Better to stamp out the embers of resistance now than rush around later with a bucket.

There was a considerable shuffling of paper while a puce Sir Merlin collected himself, patted his inside pockets looking for something and gave his tie a vicious twist.

'Pavlov. Interesting. You know that the Russians trained dogs to associate the underside of tanks with food? Had a bomb on their backs with a broom handle fuse. Hard not to sympathise with the German tank commander. I mean, we all love our dogs do we not? Difficult to shoot them but sometimes we must. Labrador man, myself.'

176

He looked Spender in the eye but the response came back immediately,

'Miss Turnbull has rescue dogs. Brown dogs, she calls them. She says that they are clever, loyal and straight.

You still haven't answered her question Sir Merlin and she hasn't got a bomb on her back. Why the interest?'

Impossible young man, thought Sir Merlin. Glib, arrogant response to a perfectly reasonable and delicately posed enquiry about this girl's credentials and motive. Time to put him in his place.

'I act for the Playfair family trust. I imagine that even you are familiar with the name?'

Spender certainly was. He had once been seduced into buying Playfair shares. He had had plenty of time since to regret his decision. The new dawn of British textiles was, it seemed, still some way below the Asian horizon.

'I am.'

'The family have long since relinquished executive control of their namesake enterprise. They are, obviously, still involved in terms of equity and tradition. However, their focus has turned to philanthropy. The arts in particular. The Playfair Institute for example.

It is a complicated trust with many branches. Direct. By marriage. By outright gift and by discretionary support.

Your client, subject to verification, falls under the first category. You will see my need for clarity.'

This Spender could see. The happy trajectory of his life had left him often underwhelmed by labels that others found impressive.

But Joy as a Playfair?

This needed the iron control of a man one length down on the Surrey station approaching Hammersmith Bridge. He had been there. He was equal to the task.

'I do see. On what grounds do you presume this connection?'

Sir Merlin began with a carefully censored account of what Joffrey had told him one year back in Edinburgh. A story of young but doomed love. A Playfair girl meeting and falling for an entirely unsuitable young man. He mentioned neither place nor date.

'Her parents, naturally, were horrified but being a close-knit family they hesitated to forbid this friendship. They tried a more subtle approach. Gentle dissuasion and the imposition of obstacles to their meeting. Luckily, they lived far apart.

Sadly, this civilised manner was lost on their daughters suitor. He seemed to have an unhealthy hold on her; was evidently poisoning her mind against her parents.

No doubt she thought that she loved him. She was young and impressionable, product of a sheltered life.

I need hardly say that a name like Playfair attracts all sorts of mendicants. Bounty hunters looking for a ready- made fortune.'

It occurred to Sir Merlin that the wicked twist he was giving his narrative was far from the sentiments that Joffrey had talked of.

If this girl really was Alice Playfair's daughter, she would inevitably meet both he and Joffrey and hear their very different accounts of the events leading to her conception. However, the two principal actors were dead and, as far as he knew, there were no others to bear witness.

Truth, he thought, is rarely absolute. One man's verity, another's charade . All depended on the prejudice and perception of the audience. The girl would have to make her own mind up. He was simply airing an alternative view. He continued.

'Sensing the resistance of her parents, the young man decided on the cads solution. He could not bear the thought that his golden goose might be waddling away.

He made her pregnant.

If he thought that this would settle the matter, he was badly mistaken. Far from tying her to him, he exposed himself for what her parents had long intimated.

All talk of a wedding was promptly cancelled. The affair terminated forthwith, and the girl sent abroad beyond his reach.

To illustrate the type of man he was, I need only say that he was very quickly married to some other unfortunate soul.

Hardly the action of a broken heart.

Meanwhile the unfortunate Miss Playfair either would not, or could not, terminate the pregnancy and a child was born. A girl.

This was a disaster for someone in her position. An illegitimate child. It would have ruined her prospects. Blighted her future life. It was immediately given up for adoption. Her parents kept no record of where or to whom. It was a deliberate policy to encourage their daughter to look forward not backwards. Everyone makes mistakes, the trick is not to brood. They were remarkably forgiving, I think.'

Spender considered the story. It seemed that he was missing something.

''Sir Merlin this is all very interesting and not something to be found, I imagine, in any official Playfair history. But what has it to do with my client? Her name is, or rather her

maiden name was, Turnbull. She never knew her father but her mother was a constant presence up to the day that she died. She lived with her, was raised by her and misses her terribly. She has photograph albums by the score to prove it. I doubt that she even knows the name Playfair, save for underwear and carpets.'

Sir Merlin looked up. He was ill at ease and chose his words carefully.

'Yes Mr Spender. My sentiments also. Will you let me continue?

Sadly for Miss Playfair her mental scars did not heal as easily as they obviously had for her one time beau.

There was one disastrous attempt at marriage after which she moved abroad and became something of a recluse.

The shock of what she had done and the shame it bought, was too much for her parents. They both died shortly after the fiasco. She was left an only child, bereft of family.

Eventually she made a new sort of life for herself; staid and spinsterly.

Her two unfortunate attempts at marriage had made her, sadly, something of a cynic in that direction. Understandable I think.

'We now, I am afraid, come to the sad end of this history.'

To Spender it seemed that the whole thing had been sad. The sad story of a wasted life. Poor little rich girl. He could not see how it could get much worse and he was still no nearer to Joy, save for wild supposition.

Sir Merlin continued. 'I am sure that you will have witnessed the phenomenon . How the elderly, sensing their three score years and ten almost up, turn to a morbid stocktaking of their achievements. What they have done and what they have left undone. A last attempt to tie up loose ends. Balance the books, so to speak'

Spender had indeed seen this type of final scramble. He shuddered to think of the various skeletons that might appear as he tried to make his own peace with his maker

'I do not know what precipitated it, but my client became obsessed with the idea of finding her child. I advised against such action. No good could come of it.'

Sir Merlin meant no good for him. He had his own firm ideas where Alice Playfair's money should go. These did not include some dredged up last minute bastard daughter.

'She would not listen to reason and there is a whole underworld that preys on the foibles of rich old women. Make their living by encouraging their fantasies and pandering to their whims.'

Spender did not point out that in his view, Sir Merlin was part of that network, albeit from its upper strata.

'Somehow Miss Playfair found and engaged the services of some self styled private investigator based here in London. This awful fellow did not hesitate to spread his unlooked for largesse around his cronies and soon my misguided client had another one

of these vultures on her books. From Switzerland can you believe? I shudder to think what it all cost.

As is their fashion, they strung her along for a while before finally turning up a name. That of Miss Turnbull, your client.

Miss Playfair became very excited, overexcited in fact, and in large part I blame these men for her untimely demise. She so wanted to believe that this girl was her long lost child.

The shock was too much for her frail constitution, despite the proof that they offered being entirely circumstantial.

A birth certificate corresponding to roughly the right time and place. A spoor, conveniently hard to verify, linking an adopted infant down the years to your client.

I am sceptical Mr Spender. Very sceptical.

It is all too convenient and, as I have said, this would not be the first attempt to hijack Miss Playfair's assets.'

It was probably more than Sir Merlin had meant to say. It was certainly unwise. Spender aroused was a crowd clearer.

He had gone pale and was silent. A bad sign. He stood. Even worse.

Both Sir Merlin and his adjutant gave their chairs an involuntary push backwards.

When he spoke his tone had none of Sir Merlin's self-important bluster. It was quiet and loaded with menace.

'Sir Merlin, the first time we met you felt fit to make snide insinuations about my business affairs. Now you start to libel my client. I find your attitude reprehensible, incomprehensible and wholly unjustified. You will retract your last comments or this meeting is over. I remind you that it was you who instigated this search; not Miss Turnbull.'

The reaction was immediate. Abject retreat. Much waving and then wringing of hands almost as if Sir Merlin expected a physical assault and was raising his arms in the universal sign of surrender.

'Mr Spender. My dear fellow. Please. You misunderstand me. I meant to cast no aspersion on the integrity of your client. She is, I am sure, entirely without blame. Unconscious of the events that I have described. But you must allow that I act in what I perceive to be my own clients best interests.

All this' daughter' business happened in a rush with no oversight or guiding hand. I could hardly be expected to have forseen the outcome; yet I must now pick up the pieces and try and make some sense of it. You must see why I am wary of confidence tricksters. See that it is my legal duty to establish identity with certainty. Examine possible motive. I owe it to the Playfair family. I owe it to the late Alice Playfair herself.'

His words seem to have a calming effect.. Spender sat down, his face a mask of concentration as if he were attempting mental long division. There was silence. Finally he looked Sir Merlin in the eye,

'Alice Playfair. You did say ALICE Playfair?'

'Yes, yes. My client, Miss Alice Playfair; or rather her estate.'

It was that eureka moment. Cortez's first glimpse of the Pacific . Enlightenment. The Alice from the letters. The 'all my love', the 'longing to be with you' Alice.

It finally made sense: but what a discovery!

A secret nearly fifty years old. A lifetime's protective magic cloak now pulled away by death.

He could hardly imagine the self-control, the limitless patience, that Matthew must have had.

The times he would have longed to unburden himself to Joy. Yet, somehow, he had resisted.

Nearly succumbed at the last it was true. Handed her a riddle not an answer. But a riddle, that once deciphered, turned the page on an entire life.

How on earth would he tell Joy?

To Sir Merlin's puzzlement, but intense relief, Spender was smiling. A happy smile, not something he had seen before.

'Well Sir Merlin, I hear what you say. 'Meaning he had listened and disagreed with most of it.

'I can indeed understand the complication that this revelation causes you. I do see the need for proof of identity. I came quite unprepared for what you have told me. I confess to being amazed and can only guess as to the reaction of my client.

If true, it rewrites the whole of her life story. She is not who she believes herself to be.

Unlike you, I am inclined to believe it.

You see, in these past few weeks I have heard and seen things that seemed to have no place in the life of Miss Turnbull as I thought I understood it.

Given the context of who she is, or perhaps I should say, appears to be, they made no sense.'

He was thinking of Matthew's box and its contents.

'It was a rather like the jigsaw puzzle of an abstract painting. You, I think, have given me the box cover with the picture painted on it. I can see now how the pieces join to make a whole.'

And, sensing a question, he held up a hand.

'Before you ask, let me show you something.'

He reached into his satchel and extracted an envelope. It contained the copies he had made of Alice's long ago letters. He handed it to a baffled Sir Merlin.

'Perhaps you will recognise the handwriting. The signature also.'

Much as Joffrey, Sir Merlin studied them intently, passing them, one by one, to the silent Justin. He appeared to be comparing them to something in the file that lay before him. At last he turned his gaze back to Spender.

'Where did you get these?'

'They were given to Miss Turnbull on the last occasion she saw the man in whose house she was raised. He was very ill, mortally as it turns out. They were in a closed canteen. He gave it to her with no mention of the contents and she did not open it until later. Too late.

What impressed her most, she has told me, is the way in which he gave her this canteen. Almost as if he were begging her to take it.

My client is not given to hyperbole, Sir Merlin. I doubt she even knows the meaning of the word. If she says that is how it was, then that is how it was.

The letters were a mystery to her. She knew no Alice, had never heard him speak the name.

It was obvious that they were love letters from a time before his marriage. She guessed that he had given them to her because they were precious to him and would have caused chaos if found by his wife. It was, I understand, a far from happy union.

If this man turns out to be who I suspect him to be, you have him wrong Sir Merlin. A gold digger doesn't hoard the evidence of profitless tailings.

They are written by Alice Playfair, are they not?'

It was a pensive Sir Merlin who finally spoke.

'Mr Spender, there are many women called Alice. I will allow you that there are certain similarities in signature and style. I am not an expert on such matters. It is to such men that we must turn for a professional opinion. They will need the originals.

Mr Spender, may I ask if the name Joffrey means anything to you? You see, I cannot understand why you thought that these letters might be germane to our business if, as you say, your client has no idea of their author.'

If he hoped to discomfort Spender by his question he was wrong.

'Miss Turnbull is my client Sir Merlin. She lives abroad. That is the main reason she is not here today. She has her own life to lead.

But yes, if you mean Mr John Joffrey of Don McCluskey and Younger WS, we are acquainted.

I met with him a fortnight ago on what I thought to be a separate matter. It now seems that they are linked, and from your question, I gather that you share the same opinion.'

They had said all that really could be said. The meeting drew to a close. Spender confirmed that he would send Joy's current details once he had her consent.

At that stage, said Spender, it would be helpful to know what exactly was involved. What Sir Merlin proposed.

After that they might meet again, probably ensemble. He could not resist a parting shot.

'Well Sir Merlin, thank you. Until the next time. Oh, and a propos of absolutely nothing, I think I'm right in saying that nightclubs are not really up your street. My club, however, sometimes doubles as a gallery. Art at lunchtime. That sort of thing. Up-and-coming sculptors, artists and photographers. Why not come and take a look? You never know, you might find a Christmas present for your wife. Good day.'

He left a floundering Sir Merlin with his private thoughts,

'So it was you. You utter, utter bastard.'

Chapter 34

The messages on his answering machine when he returned to his flat that evening were all from Joy. She wanted to hear the upshot of his meeting. She was, not unnaturally, curious about why a London lawyer was looking for her.

She also worried that somehow this link had got Spender and his nightclub into hot water. If that were the case, she knew that forgiveness would be slow and grudging. It didn't matter that she was an unwitting agent.

Spender realised that this was going to be a hard call to return. Not really a suitable subject for the impersonal medium of the telephone. He considered the alternatives. A letter, electronic or paper, meant less chance of misunderstanding and greater scope for uninterrupted explanation.

Best of all would-be face to face but not here in London. The shock of such unexpected news, its profound ramifications, would be more easily assimilated in a familiar environment.

It seemed likely that he would soon be folding his large frame into a budget airline seat for the second time in as many months.

Perhaps he should bring reinforcements. An extra target for disbelief, and who could tell, even anger, at having been deceived for so long. Johnny Laidlaw had been involved from the start of this affair. Moreover, he lived in the community that Spender suspected might soon become a scandalised battlefield. It could not hurt, he thought, to make a start in getting lined up before conflict broke out. Yes, he would ask, make, Johnny come with him.

Then there was Joffrey. Spender wagered that the mild mannered old boy had known all along, but had left him to do his own digging in order to rend the revelation more credible. The evidence of one's own eyes is easier to believe than second hand history. He would need to talk to Joffrey,

Delve further into these secrets of the past. Above all, ensure that no further bombshells would contradict what he must tell Joy.

Now he had a plan he felt easier. A holding call to Joy this evening. Next, Johnny's marching orders, with as brief an explanation as possible to get him moving.

Tomorrow he would ring Edinburgh. He hoped that he was not putting the cart before the horse, but he sensed an ally in Joffrey, sympathy toward Joy which did not conceal any nasty surprise.

'Joy? Good evening, I'm ringing to ask you to stop clogging up my telephone. What? Yes I've had the meeting. What? No I'm not pissed, I've been at work. It all went pretty well. Seems just possible that you might be in line for another handout: we've obviously strayed into Alice In Wonderland, ha, ha but I wouldn't start spending yet. Who? He was pretty cagey about that, you obviously have a secret admirer.

Important thing is that Monst is off the hook. Very good story; so good, I'm going to come and tell you in person. No, not next year; as soon as you like. Next weekend say?

Johnny Laidlaw wants to tag along, feels he might be helpful on the Scottish side, that okay?

Listen, got to rush. Dinner with Edita. No you don't know her, she's way above your class. I'll ring with flights when I booked. Got to go. Lots of love.'

And then, as if an afterthought, 'Good exhibition on at the Playfair Institute, extraordinary family. Check them out on the net. Maybe I'll treat you. Ciao.'

'Vintage Spender' thought Joy, 'verbally rush you off your feet, invite himself and his friends to stay, chuck in a snippet to keep you keen and then, all in a rush, have to go.' It had been ever thus.

She turned to her expectant husband. 'Apparently nothing. Indeed so much of nothing that he's coming in person to read my palm. Bringing Johnny L. with him, so put down that glass. You'll need your liver this weekend.'

She turned on her laptop. An exhibition in London would make a welcome change from the sheep sheds. 'Playfair,' Spender had said. She settled to read.

Johnny Laidlaw was next. He was not at home. 'Out killing something' thought Spender. He left a message telling Johnny to book himself out to France. They were staying chez Bouleau this weekend. It was to do with Joffrey and the London business. Something had come up, he would explain later, but it was vital for Joy that Johnny be there. 'You can't let her down.'

Satisfied, he took himself to bed. There was no dinner engagement, Edita was already tucked in. He would tackle Joffrey tomorrow

The telephone call left Joffrey with a dilemma. He had listened with care to what Spender had to tell him. Despite the confident tone on the other end of the line he realised that his advice was being sought. The young barrister from London had evidently joined the dotted lines; added Alice and Matthew and arrived at Joy.

If Sir Merlin pretended to doubt the credentials of Spenders client, he did not. The girl must be told the truth and the sooner the better.

The secret was still contained within the legal trio. His experience suggested that this confined space would soon expand. At first by single whispered confidence which, when repeated, gathered a momentum of its own.

He had made a promise to Matthew. That promise was here in his office in the form of a sealed envelope.

His promise was that Matthew, and no one else, would tell Joy her true history. Explain how it had come about and give the reasons why it had taken so long to be revealed.

Joffrey was not a particularly religious man, but he believed in honouring the dead. More so if they had been steadfastly honourable in life, and concerned a man that he had been proud to call his friend.

The choices open to him were several. Spender had not told him Joy's name or address. Nor thank God, had he told Sir Merlin. The conduit was therefore Spender, but how to use him?

The coward's route would be simply to let Spender

recount what he had learned. This, he did not even consider.

A second possibility would be to send the envelope, along with an explanation written by himself, via Spender.

This method would not breach the letter of his obligation but, he felt, nor would it honour the spirit in which it had been given. After all, he thought, the sealed words, though coming from Matthew's heart, had been, in places, gently coached; he supplying order and sequence to the raw emotion.

No. He was certain that he should be there in person when the seal was broken. It would be quite hard enough anyway. The girl deserved better than to face it alone.

He returned Spenders call as he had promised and announced his decision. Spender did not seem surprised.

'Mr Spender, I have long anticipated this day. I had hoped that the passage of time might lighten the burden of what must be laid at the feet of your client. I had not counted on the continuing venality of a wife, nor that one in particular of her daughters would breed so true to type.

You have, no doubt, heard some of the lurid detail from Mr Laidlaw.

At our last meeting I mentioned a letter of explanation from my client to yours. You can now guess at its general content.

I also said that I had had a hand in its drafting. This letter was to be opened after the death of my client's wife and before the estate was wound up.

That time, it seems, is now.

I have considered whether to entrust this letter to you for onward conveyance to your client. I would prefer not to. It would, I think, be unfair to you both. While the contents are self explanatory, there are bound to be questions.

My client was a private man and I believe that I am the only person left alive who knows exactly what happened. The when and the where.

Perhaps I flatter myself, but I think that I might also offer some insight as to the 'why'.

He had Spenders full agreement. Any articulate mechanic

can explain the workings of an engine. Deeper insight requires something else, witness or priest perhaps. Joffrey was the former and Spender, certainly no priest.

He asked the question.

'Mr Joffrey, I know this is an imposition, but would you be prepared to accompany me when I visit Miss Turnbull? I plan to go this weekend; news like this has a short shelf life.'

It was what Joffrey had hoped for, despite the lack of forewarning. Golf at Mussleburgh would have to wait and, he brightened. Mrs Joffrey was always hinting at a weekend break. Two birds with one stone. It appealed to his parsimonious Scottish mind.

The details were quickly settled. The Joffreys would find space in some nearby country hotel. He would rent a car and take that modern tool, a mobile phone, with him. When Spender called he would come. It was then, he thought, that any holiday mood might end.

Chapter 35

It was one of those lovely October weekends that, by their rarity, count as a news item in England. In the centre of France, whilst appreciated by the residents, it passed without much comment.

Perou was looking at its autumnal best. After a long hot summer the September rains had washed the fields, turning everything back to green from their August khaki. The leaves on the Oak and Lime trees had matured to their respective ochre and yellow, with a carpet of white and lilac cyclamen below.

Lazy butterflies and frenetic wasps moved between the Apple trees, building their reserves of sugar for the harsher times to follow. The dogs lay in the sun.

It was only the humans, with their concentrated air of solemnity, who seemed at odds with the hot afternoon. As if they alone had already been touched by the first frosts of winter.

Spender and Johnny had arrived on the Friday evening. While animated, there had been something forced about their gaiety, a slightly fin-de-ciecle atmosphere, as if nothing would ever be quite the same again.

Both Joy and Mick had sensed the mood but neither of their guests would be drawn on what it presaged.

Just before bed Spender took Joy aside.

'Joy, I'm afraid that I have taken a certain liberty with your hospitality. You know who I mean by Joffrey, the Edinburgh solicitor?'

As if she might not, thought Joy.

'Well I have asked him to come over too. He's here in France, slumming it in some nearby hotel with his wife. He can explain much better than me what this is all about and he has something to show you. It was as much his idea as mine and I think that you'll like him. Things have happened, but that's for tomorrow. Anyway, we both thought it better not to delay. Don't lose any sleep over it. As I said before, it's good news if a little complicated.

May he come over tomorrow, in the afternoon say?'

The roller coaster was truly speeding up if even Spender could not apply the brakes, Joy realised. Her reply however, was as Spender had anticipated. He received a thorough ticking off.

She was horrified, she said, that the poor man had been banished to the dubious world of Limousin hotels. She hadn't seen a decent one yet. Why on earth had he not invited him to stay here? There was plenty of space and decent baths; not the fiddly little French tubs.

He should have told her earlier, after all, she was in his hands.

If the reason for Joffrey's presence was good enough for him, it would do for her. Now she just looked standoffish.

Certainly invite him over, but make it for lunch. Both of them, husband and wife. It would give her time to get to know the man a little. He in turn, could see who Joy was ,and something of how she lived.

Ring him first thing tomorrow she said.

It was a chastened but heartened Spender who climbed into bed after vain attempts to escape the accompanying terrier. Joy was in fighting form. Anxious, but not dreading the events of tomorrow. It would be a shock, of that he was sure. But a shock with money attached is easier to accept than its naked alternative.

'My goodness she's like Matthew,' Joffrey thought. Not so much in appearance, although from certain angles he could see a resemblance. More in character. An outgoing, welcoming personality. Fun never far from the surface.

Yet her lifestyle also spoke of privacy and a self-reliant reserve. He should know, he had been trying to find her for long enough, after all.

He had last seen her at that awkward stage between girl and woman, and no one looks their best at the funeral of someone they love.

This finished article, he knew, would have delighted Matthew.

Lunch had been taken outside on the parterre under the lime trees. Joy and he had talked of the old days; Matthew and Gladdies. They both avoided the present. Joffrey had allowed himself a few more glasses than usual while Spender, Johnny and Mick regaled his wife with the usual silly stories of misadventure and penance. After cheese and fruit Spender had stood, ordered Joy to make coffee, and announced that they had better get down to business.

'Johnny why don't you take Mrs Joffrey on a tour of the policies? I'm sure Mick won't begrudge the use of his Land Rover. That way you'll get round the whole lot.'

The message was clear. Go away, and don't come back for some time.

'Joy what do you want Mick to do? There's plenty of washing up and that delicious Armagnac that he almost single-handedly demolished, needs replacing. Oh and get some Fizz while you're at it. We might need it later.'

And then he did that very rare thing for Spender. He pressed a bundle of notes into Mick's hand.

'He's more nervous than me.' Thought Mick, 'but never look a gift horse in the mouth.'

All he said was, 'Yes bass' in his best South African accent and then, to his wife, 'I won't be far away if you need me.'

They went their various ways. Mick to the kitchen, the walkers to the courtyard and the legal party to the dining room. Joffrey did not miss the meaningful glance from his wife. They had few secrets between them and she knew what this was all about. Her look said, 'this is a good girl. Tread gently.' It was advice that he did not need, but it is always comforting to have one's spouse share one's views.

They sat down around one end of the dining room table, Joffrey at the head. It was a long, thin room hung with works by Joy and peopled by somnolent, buzzing flies. Spender broke the silence.

'Joy this is Mr Joffrey's story not mine. He will tell it

192

better than I can. If at any stage you are unclear or want to stop, just say so. Likewise if you want to talk to your husband or to me alone, I'm sure that Mr Joffrey will understand. Ready?'

Joy nodded her assent and Joffrey began.

'Mrs Bouleau or Joy as you have kindly asked me to call you. I want to start by giving you a letter. It is from Matthew. From our lunchtime conversation, you will have gathered that we were friends.

I am not sure when he set down the first draft, but this final version was written in 1992. I know this because he sought my advice on some of the content, and entrusted its safekeeping to my firm.

These are not the words of a man making a deathbed confession although he knew that he did not have much time left. It was to be passed to you after the death of his wife Andrea.

Had she predeceased him, it was to be returned to him unopened and I have no doubt he would have told you its contents in person.

I promised him that I would give it to you without comment beforehand. Please read it and I will try and answer any questions that you may have.'

Joy took the proffered envelope. It was creased and reused with Matthew's own name and address roughly crossed out and the single word 'Joy' written in black ink on the front. As had been Matthew's wont, it was sealed with red wax embossed with the mark of his battered old signet ring; a snarling wolf. It was also heavy. There was obviously more than paper inside.

Hesitantly she turned the envelope around, examining both sides, squeezing and trying to guess the contents. Then she broke the seal, taking care that the wax imprint was left undamaged.

A single white feather was stuck to the inside of the wax. There were more in the envelope. The downy remains of long dead hens and peafowl. Matthew had always loved his poultry and every letter she had ever received from him contained feathers. Their private language, his secret joke.

193

There were also two rings.

The tears started.

'I'm sorry but please could you both go outside. I would like to read this alone and I don't want to embarrass either you or me by blubbing.'

Chapter 36

For Matthew, it was a long letter.

'My darling Joy, I had always hoped that this was something that you would not have to read. I know now that you will. The doctors are gloomy. I think that they are right.

It's only a few days since you came to see me. It seems an age.

I hope that you got that old silver canteen safely home. The money is yours, my love. It is not enough compared to what I want to give, but there should be more to come.

My old friend, John Joffrey, or someone from his firm if he is unable, will tell you how.

I want to tell you about your mother. You know how fond I always was of Mrs Turnbull. She was an exceptional woman. By far the most intelligent person, bar perhaps you, at Gladdies and an integral part of the family.

She loved you very, very deeply and was always so proud of you.

I still have no idea how to say what I now must. Mrs Turnbull and I often thought about it, discussed how it might be done. I am still none the wiser. All I can do is state the bald facts.

You were born on 25 May 1963 at a nursing home in Basle, Switzerland. Not Glasgow.(So you're not really a Scot! Bad luck.)

Your mother was called Alice Playfair; not Margaret Turnbull. I am your father.'

Joy stopped reading, as much for the sense of bewilderment, as for the tears that blurred her vision. She reached down to touch the small brown dog that lay at her side. If he was there, then this must be real. Not a dream. She looked again at the last few lines. They too were still there. Still stating their extraordinary news. She wiped her eyes and read on.

'Alice and I were engaged to be married. We had met

during the time that I was in Cirencester. You won't to be amazed to hear that it was on the hunting field.

She wrote the letters in the canteen. Bar one, you have them all, every single one that she ever wrote to me. Now they are yours and you know why.

I loved her very much. I think the letters show that she felt the same. I did not know about you until far too late.

I wish with all my heart that I had known. I would not have acted as I did. No use crying over spilt milk as your grandmother used to say. She, on the other hand, knew exactly who you were but I'm jumping the gun.

One day I got a letter. It was from Alice's father. She had had second thoughts, he said and while still fond of me, no longer wished to get married.

The father, not your cup of tea or mine, said that he agreed with his daughter. That while I might be disappointed, I should take the news like a man. Think of what was right for Alice and generally get on with my life. He enclosed a letter from Alice. It's the one you haven't got. I burnt it and threw the ashes in the loch.

I didn't, and still don't, believe that they were her own sentiments. I think the text was dictated and the signature forced. I think that it was her parents who rejected me, not her. They were fussy, prissy people and I wasn't grand enough for them.

I tried to find her, but Alice had disappeared. Switzerland as I much later discovered. Her parents certainly weren't going to tell me. Nor did I know that you were on the way. To my lasting shame, I gave up.

About one year later, I was paying my Sunday visit to my mother. You remember them, lunch and a stroll in the garden. There was an atmosphere. I was given a large glass of sherry and firmly sat down in the drawing room. I wondered what I'd done. You can perhaps imagine how the news of your existence was broken. A no-nonsense granny fait accompli. This is the gist of it.

You had been born and immediately whisked away. I don't know whether Alice even held you; I think not. The idea seems to have been, sooner gone, sooner forgotten.

196

Alice, brave girl, had managed to get the news that she was pregnant to my mother. My mother had not replied but evidently she plotted.

Mrs Turnbull had asked for two weeks holiday. She said she wanted to visit relatives in the South. I didn't think anything of it: heaven knows, she was due some time off.

What she had not said was that she was in cahoots with my mother and en route to Basle where a baby was waiting for her. You. She later told me that it was the only time she ever took an aeroplane and that she hadn't thought much of the experience.

How my mother fixed it all, she never told me. Mrs Turnbull found you neatly packaged and ready to go, paperwork and everything. Poor Mrs Turnbull wasn't given a choice, perhaps you can remember how imposing my mother could be.

Actually she was thrilled. She doted on you right from the start.

Anyway, while I was still reeling from this news, Mrs Turnbull was wheeled in, grinning like a Cheshire cat, and I first set eyes on you. I would like to say that you looked like Alice. You do now. Back then you resembled a slightly squashed peach, you were the first baby that I had ever seen close-up. Your two half sisters started off much the same.

I had better talk about them. They will be just as shocked as I imagine you are by all this. They may be reluctant to believe, especially Petronella, she was always jealous of you.

I told her that the basis of our bond was shared interest. Now you know there was more to it than that.

I have written to both of them explaining what happened. I hope that they will accept it.

I have never told Andrea, and I hope that she will never find out. I have asked John Joffrey to use his discretion as to when to give you this letter, but if possible to wait until Andrea could no longer be affected. She would have been terribly hurt.

She knew of Alice in a general sort of way, but hated the fact that I had been engaged to someone else before her.

Lots and lots of broken china, I think, if she found out about you.

Both my mother and Mrs Turnbull were dead against telling you.

I hope this explains why I haven't told you before. It was for your protection, for Mrs Turnbull's protection, and so that peace, such as it is, can reign in this house.

Perhaps I have been wrong. I hope that you can forgive me .I find it hard to forgive myself.

And so to the future. I hope that you're happy. I hope that you find, or have found someone to love. I hope that you have children. I'm willing to bet that you have dogs and horses, I can't imagine you without.

The farm belongs to Andrea for her life. She has promised me that she will remember you in her will, even if she thinks it an odd request.

I have left you the picture on the stairs and some shares which, I'm told, have promise.

If you have any say in the matter, don't hesitate to sell Gladdies. Land has no emotion and nor should you.

What was in the canteen is for you alone.

I have put two rings in this letter. My old signet ring. As you are my oldest child it is right that it should go to you. You've probably guessed where the diamond one comes from. It is the engagement ring that I gave to Alice. She returned it with that awful letter. I very nearly threw it into the loch as well; too mean, I suppose. Now I'm glad that I didn't.

Finally, Alice. Perhaps you will want to find her, see your real mother with your own eyes. Knowing you, I think you will. It was not her fault that you were taken from her.

Tell her your story, show her the ring, expect disbelief. She was never told where you went. I didn't expect to have to wait this long. Be patient, she is an old lady now and, I'm sure, will be furious with me.

You are the proof that I never forgot, never stopped missing her. She will, I think, understand that.

That's really all there is to say and I am getting tired. I am so, so sorry my darling.

Perhaps we'll meet again somewhere else. I hope so.

Remember that I've always loved you and always will and, at last, something I've longed to write,

Daddy.

Joy stopped reading. It seemed as if time too had stopped. Carefully she shuffled the sheets of paper into their correct order, gently smoothing the creases she had made. Epiphany. A word much used, rarely experienced. The information contained in this capsule from the past was just that.

Overwhelming. Changing all that she had supposed about herself into something new and strange. Wonderful, even.

Her own father was no longer some phantom of her imagination. He was a real man. Flesh and blood who she had known and loved.

That special bond between them had been rooted in something much deeper than mere sentiment.

So unbelievable that it had to be true. A magical transformation from base metal to gold. From humble to noble, from housekeeper's girl to laird's daughter.

She reached down again. The dog was still there. It was not a dream.

She stood up and went through to where Spender and Joffrey were waiting. They looked as shy as she felt. As if she were again a little girl, intruding on the adult world.

All she said was,

'Sorry. Sorry to have kept you waiting so long.'

She called for her husband, took him by the arm and led him back into the dining room. Seeing the alarm on his face she smiled and kissed him

'You had better read this. I'm afraid that you've married an imposter' and then, enigmatically,' Poor, poor mum.'

Mick took the sheets of paper and read in silence. Normally he devoured words. Here he was slow, continually turning back as if for confirmation. Normally he gave a running commentary as he read. Matthew had silenced him. Finally he finished, stunned.

'What next?'

'I suppose we'd better talk to the messengers. Don't go

away. I'm feeling rather odd' came the answer. 'You're my reality check' and she kissed him again. 'Could you go and get them?'

They came back in, the older man first and found their chairs with that awkwardness that emotion brings to professional men. It was Mick rather than Joy who spoke. The question was abrupt but it was asked gently.

'How long have you known about this?'

Despite being directed at Spender it was Joffrey who replied.

'For far too long I am afraid. My hands were somewhat tied by the conditions that Matthew had imposed and by the robust constitution, despite her constant denial of the fact, enjoyed by Andrea.

Then came the problem of finding you, Joy. Thanks to Mr Spender and Mr Laidlaw, that was achieved rather more quickly.'

'I only found out the other day.' Put in Spender in a slightly affronted tone.

They all waited for Joy.

'I don't think it matters' she said quietly,' it all started long ago and what's done is done. A month here or there changes nothing. Nor, at the moment, do I feel changed. It's as if I've been reading about someone else.

I accept that it is true, only Matthew could have written like that. It just doesn't seem' and she searched for the right word, 'well; relevant. I'm still Mrs Bouleau , Perou is still my home. I'm still a mother. I still paint. The children will be fascinated. I'm sure I will too, later on. I'm sorry. I hope that you don't think I'm being rude.'

'Not even slightly' said Joffrey with a smile. 'Your reaction makes perfect sense to me. I'm sure that I would feel the same. Nothing has changed save, if you wish, some words on a birth certificate.

I very much hope, without, I am bound to say ,great expectation, that certain others will see it in the same vein.'

Petronella and Elsa, Matthew's two other daughters. The thought of them, what they would say and do, especially Petronella, suddenly made her new status clear to Joy. She

200

could continue as before. Hidden. But that was surely cowardice.

Nonetheless, fighting with a drunk or lunatic and Petronella fitted both labels, often simultaneously, is rarely profitable. She looked at Joffrey.

'I know that it is an awful thing to ask, but do I have to be there when whatever happens, the reading if that's what it's called, takes place?'

There was a gentle chuckle from Joffrey.

'Only if you want to be. You might choose to send an ambassador in your stead. Your lawyer for example. As a barrister, Mr Spender is a keen student of human theatre. I'm sure that he would appreciate the show.'

Spender nodded his assent. He had not met Petronella before, but had heard Johnny's stories. He knew a poisoned chalice when he was handed one, but could hardly desert as the guns began to sound.

Joy had a second question. Again it was addressed to Joffrey although it was more properly within Spenders domain.

'And what about the London end. This Mr Hayley?'

Both Joffrey and Spender enjoyed the demotion but gently corrected the fault. It would do her no good to antagonise the man.

'Sir. Sir Merlin Hayley, Joy. I'm afraid that he's rather apt to stand on ceremony, especially where it concerns him.'

'I see no real need for an immediate personal visit in his case either' Joffrey continued.

'Eventually you may want to meet him but for now we two should be able to cope.

I suspect that any legacy from your mother, Alice Playfair, will be more complicated than Matthew's affairs. It is a large family and I believe their individual accounts are bundled together under the umbrella of a common trust. In any event, I will inform Sir Merlin we have made contact. When we know more, you can decide how to proceed.

For my part, once I have discharged my duty to Matthew, I should be honoured to act for you in your private capacity should you so wish; our legal customs north of the border differ from Mr Spender's area of expertise.'

'Can't resist touting for business' thought Spender, although he simply said, 'That would probably be sensible, Joy.'

Their musings were cut short by the rattling of Mick's Land Rover as Johnny negotiated the farm road at his customary speed. Joy looked out of the dining room window. Mrs Joffrey appeared to be entranced, but then Johnny had always been a hit with the girls.

'Time I think for a drink. We mustn't waste the weather. Spends, could you do the honours? Johnny's certainly going to need one when he hears what I have got to say.'

The evening was a relatively sober affair. The Joffreys were persuaded to stay for dinner although they declined the offer of a bed. Johnny had put on his serious face when Joy drew him aside.

He professed himself less than amazed by the revelation. The whole Gladdies set up, he said, had seemed fishy; although Joy could not recall these sentiments being aired before. As it happened he knew some Playfairs. East Anglia. Delightful people, pretty daughter. Shot there once or twice. Funny to think that Joy was related to them. He'd have to get them together.

In truth Johnny was surprised. Very surprised. He couldn't wait to see Petronella's reaction. Dumfriesshire society was in for a treat.

Joy spent most of the evening in quiet conversation with Joffrey. There would be questions, she knew, that would occur to her later.

He rehearsed her on what to expect from her share of the estate and confirmed that, as he had thought, bearer certificates meant nothing to her, and portraits of Victorian gentleman were no more than vague childhood memories.

He would contact both she and Spender once he had tied down her two sisters to a date. Money was for later. He could not predict time or amount and the tax man would want his share.

As to what he called chattels, furniture, silver and the like, he was less certain.

'I am afraid that against my council Matthew left the farm and household contents to Andrea. She has been a regular customer for the Edinburgh sale rooms. What's left, and there must be some, has often, quite literally, Petronella's name inscribed on it. Your half sister is a very persuasive lady. In Andrea's defence, I don't think that she had much choice in the matter.'

Joy listened to this without rancour. Gladdies, once her home, had slowly receded to mixed memories. Without Matthew, it meant nothing to her and she had never associated him with the indoor world of Andrea.

Money seemed similarly unreal. She had never known a time when money, or its lack, didn't tiptoe at the back of her mind.

Perhaps this would mean an end to those four am panics. A cautious opening to a world of more than strictly useful presents. Bankers who smile rather than frown ,and all the quiet calm that financial security brings with it. Perhaps. She would believe it when she saw it.

As for the revelation concerning who she was: well breeding has always been an inexact science. Her own experience led her to place more emphasis on nurture than nature.

Chapter 37

The run up to Christmas is often a quiet period in the legal world. Outstanding business settled quickly, or at any rate, faster than usual. The focus shifts to the coming holiday, the slack week afterwards and prospects for the year ahead.

It was with this beguiling tone that Spender had persuaded Joy to visit London and make Sir Merlin's acquaintance. She would have to one day. Better to go now; prevarication only makes things harder, he said.

He had enjoyed less success with this line of argument where Edinburgh was concerned. He would be a lonely lawyer in a hostile world the day after next.

Still, he reasoned, a good argument would put him in fighting form for the festive family get-together. With his brother and new girlfriend also coming, a little practice would not go amiss.

It was a different Sir Merlin who greeted them when they presented themselves at his chambers. Ushering them into his office in person and without delay.

Gone was the bantam cockerel, in its stead, a wise, avuncular figure. Sober and slightly sad. It was a disguise that Spender had not seen before and he took a professional interest in how it was done.

Only the odd calculating glance betrayed the real man behind the mask.

There was the expected foreplay of unctuous regret for the circumstances of the meeting. The avowal of high regard for Joys presumed mother, and expression of pleasure and relief that Joy had been finally found.

They had been sat, not around a table, as with Joffrey. But in front of Sir Merlin's imposing desk, much in the manner of naughty schoolchildren. He hoped to intimidate.

All this had been predicted remarkably accurately the night before by Spender. He called it legal Valium. The specific numbing of awareness into which the meat of the matter would be cunningly inserted; cloaked by the surrounding flannel. 'Guff' was the word he used.

'Look beyond the fake sentiment for facts. Sift out figures, dates and places. Examine signatures,' he said. 'Demand clear English in place of trustee -speak and always remember that he is the servant and you are the master. I will only interrupt if he gets too obscure or bumptious.'

This, Joy doubted and in any event, Spender had a famously low bumption threshold.

The meeting inched forward, Sir Merlin moving gradually from platitude to specific. Alice Playfair's assets, he said, were semi-liquid but realisable within a reasonable time frame.

'He means, sell to raise cash,' Spender said.

Outwardly unruffled by this crude translation, Sir Merlin continued.

'Miss Playfair was for many years a resident of the Channel Island of Jersey. Unfortunately her house, together with its contents ,were sold shortly after her death. Given the doubt as to your whereabouts, indeed in some quarters, your actual existence, it seemed a reasonable thing to do.'

'Which quarters?'Joy watched Spender write, in letters large enough to be visible to Sir Merlin at the other side of the desk.

'The bulk of the proceeds from these sales have been added to her portion of the Playfair Family Trust. This is a rather complicated vehicle encompassing all the main branches of the family.

Her will, of which this is a copy for you, states her provisional intention to leave this portion to her only child, or offspring of that child, should she or they be discovered. Given certain formalities this may mean you.'

'What formalities?' Went down on Spenders pad.

'As you may appreciate, this is a large trust, administered for sake of ease and economy as a single entity. Individual ownership is by way of units, much as those as in a standard Unit Trust. From time to time these units can be realised.'

'Again, sold for cash.' This from Spender.

'But there are always implications, tax and otherwise, for the remaining unit holders. Therefore, for reasons of efficiency and sheer good manners, the trust has an unwritten code of conduct which I do my humble best to oversee.'

'Locked in?' Wrote Spender.

'I trust that this brief description makes clear the nature of what may be yours. Perhaps you have questions?'

This remark was directed at Joy. It was Spender who answered. Despite his earlier promise of abstinence, the glib and condescending fashion in which Sir Merlin had delivered his information drove him to it.

'Two questions immediately spring to mind, Sir Merlin.

First. You spoke earlier of formalities. I take this to mean that you have some doubt as to my client's identity. Second. I am sure that we would both be helped by figures. There is a world of difference between pennies and pounds.'

'Indeed there is Mr Spender. Indeed there is. I am afraid that it is my duty to caution you against unrealistic expectations. As I hope I have explained, Miss Playfair was the only child of a wealthy, even very wealthy, family.

Unfortunately this often goes hand in hand with expensive tastes, and gainful employment was rare among women of that class and generation.

Miss Playfair was no exception. Indeed she had a generous nature and singular penchant for charity. You see my drift. No well is bottomless, and without a clear line of succession, other worthy causes took centre stage. You will notice in her will that her choice was catholic, but tended mainly to horses, dogs and orphanages.' And with false piety,' the latter, I'm sure, you will approve.'

Spender lifted the copy of Alice's will. It was a thick wedge of densely worded paper, loosely bound with black ribbon. He started to read. Meanwhile Sir Merlin continued.

'As to the formalities that I spoke of, you must forgive me for being blunt. While personally I have no doubts as to Miss Turnbull's bona fides, others will require more substantial proof. In the language of the courtroom, the evidence is circumstantial. It is not unknown for the issue of foreign birth certificates and deeds of adoption to be less rigorously administered than is the case here. As ever, the bigger the prize, the greater the incentive.'

A very level stare from Spender bought some of the customary bluster back to Sir Merlin's voice.

'My dear fellow, it would be remiss of me not to make this point. I cast no aspersion on your client, merely state what other members of the Trust will say.

You have furnished no official British documents. I have only a letter, which a Scottish colleague assures me is genuine, from your client's father. Where I see truth and a long injustice righted, others will suspect malice or mistake. What would you have me do?'

'Would a blood test satisfy those doubting others? The initials' DNA 'convince them that their pot of gold is not being diluted by a carpetbagger? Would you do that Joy?'

'If I must,' she said.

'Please. Please. I hope that won't be necessary. I shall use my best efforts to calm the voices of suspicion. Let us move on to specifics. As I have said, what may become Miss Turnbull's property is measured in units. In this case, one hundred and ten of them. The value of each unit is a function of their underlying investments and changes in line with their respective rise and fall. At present, one unit is worth somewhere between nine hundred and one thousand pounds. The market is being rather capricious at present, as I am sure you are aware.

This being the case, I have advised all my unit holders against realisation unless absolutely necessary. There will surely be better occasions ahead and the interest of all participants must be considered. The price of some of the smaller underlying securities is sensitive to any sudden movement.'

'Illiquid.' Wrote Spender.

So that was it thought Joy. Perhaps one hundred thousand pounds. It seemed to be a recurring figure in her life. She could not help but feel disappointed. So much talk of the plutocratic Playfairs. She had dared to hope for more. Judging by the look on his face, Spender was of the same opinion. Joffrey, she felt, would also be surprised. The family were friends of Johnny Laidlaw, for heaven's sake, and he was not known for courting paupers.

Still, she rationalised, fairy tales are for children and she must not be greedy. It was a large amount of money and, allied to the Scottish sum, would make an appreciable difference to Perou and her family.

The meeting ended. Spender would study the will, but he did not think that Joy would be needed in the immediate future. He was surprised by the figures. What Sir Merlin had said was all perfectly plausible, but given the nature of the man, his scrutiny of the small print would be more than usually rigorous.

Spender was right to suspect Sir Merlin .Despite what he had stated, he had already seen both birth and adoption certificates. He had buried them deep in his personal files.

He was confident that the will would stand up. The only witness to the last minute changes was his Jersey associate, a man with much to lose and nothing to gain by any rebuttal of his signature. After all, the slurred speech of an elderly, dying stroke victim is notoriously hard to interpret, and deathbed alterations to long-standing arrangements not unknown.

He had nothing to fear, he decided. True, he had foregone a token amount to purchase peace. The bulk was where he had long since planned. It would take a very clever accountant indeed to unravel the mezzanine layers and circuitous routes by which he was linked to three of Alice Playfair's preferred charities. The fact that his wife's mothers maiden name was Playfair was pure coincidence.

Mr Spender might suspect. Proof was another matter altogether.

Chapter 38

It was one day later, another capital city, another set of meeting rooms. The same language but a culture separated by more than mere miles.

Perhaps it was the increased latitude thought Spender. Here there was no Thames Embankment with its polyglot bustle and sense of possibility. In its stead, the grey slopes of Edinburgh. The measured tread of serious men.

A town where youth knew its place, and apprenticeship was still the path to office.

But thanks to the weekend in France he now counted Joffrey as confederate, almost friend. An asset always useful when in enemy territory.

Joy and he had spent the previous night at Kirkstiel with Johnny Laidlaw. There had been a dinner party, Joy's childhood circle re-united. At first it had been pregnant with the knowledge of a shared secret; Johnny had evidently been generous with his new intelligence.

It had quickly climbed to celebration and the general delight that comes with proximity to new celebrity.

After breakfast Spender had left Joy to the serious business of fox hunting on a horse Johnny described as an' armchair.' The same term could not be applied to the car that Johnny had lent him, but in any event, he was here in the offices of Don McCluskey and Younger WS.

The cast was assembled. Joffrey resigned, Elsa quiet and nervous. A thin tweedy, pipe-cleaner of a man from a country practice in Moffat, Andrea's solicitor, and Spender himself, enjoying the tension and trying to guess Petronellas weight.

Petronella. Like some byzantine pasha she had made her entrance. Designed to awe, it had been more pantomime dame.

Starting from the top, a large, furry hat that had seen better days. A suggestion of mange. War paint on an angry face; carmine lipstick unevenly applied; patchy dabs of powder. A 1980s power cardigan, stitched together with encrusted gold buttons, one of them missing. Underneath, a grubby pink cotton polo neck faithfully following the contours of her chicken skin neck.

A sack-like ankle length skirt of some indeterminable material, rounded off by suede booties that seemed to suffer from the same disease as her hat. A once expensive handbag with overflowing contents completed the ensemble, and enveloping all was the smell of ancient scent, cigarettes, alcohol and sweat.

Spender was entranced.

The battle started in slow motion. In dry and impartial tones Joffrey gave the preamble, then moved to the will itself.

'Like something from a bad 1950s film,' thought Spender. Nonetheless, he could see that this dry dullness might blunt the initial fury of Petronella.

It didn't. To no one's surprise the caisson broke. Although noisy, it was mild in comparison with what was to come.

'Why, in God's name, is my father leaving anything to the cook's daughter? What a load of complete crap. You're making it up as you go along. Let me see that now! I know all about crooked lawyers. Bribe you did she? In it together? Sex for cash? Total and utter crap. What the fuck are you smiling at? Who are you anyway? I'm not fucking paying for you.'

This was directed at Spender who could barely resist clapping. A connoisseur, he thoroughly appreciated a good bout of hysterics.

The flow, temporarily abated, Joffrey continued.

'These are letters written by your father. He instructed me to give you them after he had made known his intentions. I think you will find the answer to your questions therein.'

Silence descended as both sisters started to read. Spender watched, fascinated.

It was like a biology test at school. Two subjects, same breeding, reared the same way. Compare and contrast. It had, however, never been this easy. To the left, Widow Twanky, already flushed, now turning from pomegranate to pimento.

To the right, Sleeping Beauty, already pale, now turning snowdrop white.

Elsa spoke first,

'Is this really true? Joy my half sister? Why didn't he tell us?'

One glance at her sister, the slower reader, would have supplied the answer. Joffrey hastened to use the interval between eruptions.

'Certainly it is true. I am proud to say that I counted your father as a friend. Lies had no part in his make-up. However, he would go to great lengths to protect the vulnerable. Dumfriesshire was not then as broad minded as it is now. Illegitimacy was bad enough for a boy. It was unthinkable for a girl. That is why.'

To Spender's unbounded admiration, Joffrey then stood. His Methodist background came to the fore, and perhaps it needed an Old Testament prophet to face the bulging volcano opposite.

'Do not speak to me of deceit, Mrs De Haan. Where are the portraits of your ancestors? Where are your father's personal effects? His stud buttons? His cuff links? His furniture, his silver? Where is his personal correspondence, his passport, his share certificates, his diaries?

Who are you to claim title over all this? To try and steal his very soul?'

This biblical denunciation had a peculiar effect on Petronella. Her bloodshot eyes stared with a mad hatred at Joffrey and Spender. Her body went rigid while her hands trembled with an epileptic palsy and her teeth ground together.

Specks of yellow bubbly foam flecked the corners of her mouth and for a long moment she seemed incapable of speech.

Then with a sharp crack; the splintering of coffee cup and saucer on the table, the spell broke.

She struggled to her feet, relieving her unfortunate chair

of its oderous burden and, thought Spender, actually started rather well. It did not last long.

'You contemptible little man. How dare you speak to me like this? I am the oldest, the first born. Perhaps your evident lack of education excuses you from knowing what primogeniture means. Let me explain.'

The volume was rapidly increasing and while thoroughly enjoying himself Spender took the precaution of placing both hands on his file, ready to shield himself from what he was sure would soon be incoming crockery.

'It means that I am the sole heir by natural right. Too complicated? It means I get everything. Everything without exception. All of it. It's all mine. The family lives on through me. Everybody, the whole world, apart from you, you chippy caledonian caveman, understands the principle.. It's the principle that has made us great. Great Britain. So don't you dare to lecture me on something beyond your pygmy comprehension.'

It was now a full-blooded scream. 'I hope that someone calls the fire brigade' thought Spender.

'Don't ask me where the family furniture is. It is with the family. With me. As to some hideous Victorian art. It's gone, broken, burnt, used as a dart board, I don't know. They weren't my family anyway, just some ghastly little people from trade. No breeding. Why should I guard their memory?

My father's personal effects, his silver? With me where they belong. Even my moronic mother could see that. Look at her will; it's all written down. It's mine.'

And to Andrea's cowering lawyer,' Show them you useless little man.'

'Passports, certificates, documents? All waste paper, all burnt. My parents were too lazy to clean and tidy up . As always, it fell to me to do it. The only child that cared. The only child that stayed close. The only real family they had.

The Turnbull slut my half sister? She's nothing. A nobody's daughter. You must think me really stupid to fall for such utter rubbish. Sell Gladdies? Over my dead body. I know you bloody lawyers. Trying to feather your own nest. Well I call it theft and I'll see you in court!'

212

With a magnificent double handed stroke, Petronella's handbag swept the contents of the table onto the carpet. She hurled her chair to one side and seized the door handle.

Unfortunately this splendid exit was somewhat spoiled by the fact that the door opened inward and not away from her as she had assumed.

This was too much for Spender, and he broke into delighted laughter while using his file to deflect the vase that came hurtling his way.

The silence in the room was punctuated by the slamming of doors as Petronella made her way out of the building and then it was over, Spender still smiling, the rest holding their breath.

It was Joffrey who came to their rescue. In a gentle voice he asked,

'I wonder if she even knows how to spell the word, contemptible?'

And then to his Scottish colleague, 'Clifford, might we see and have your thoughts on this famous Will please?'

Copies of Andrea's Will were circulated but it was immediately obvious that no comfort would be found there.

It was very simple as her lawyer explained. Andrea, although undeniably pretty and amusing when she chose, had been a vain and weak woman.

Thanks to Matthew's generosity, she became, for the first time in her life, wealthy. Although she had not realised it, and would have never acknowledged it if she had, Matthew had been her firewall. A protective barrier between Andrea, her domineering mother and her grasping daughter. When that wall fell, she found herself defenceless and the vultures moved in, fighting between themselves. While the mother extracted cash which was distributed with all the largesse of one who has not earned it, Petronella started on the material side. If not stripped bare, the infrequent visitors to Gladdies could hardly fail to notice the steady depletion of ornament and furniture.

The mother, as often seems the case with really evil

people, lasted into a ripe and vigorous old age, even receiving her telegram from the Queen before finally conceding defeat.

Now completely alone, Andrea was easy prey for Petronella with her persuasive mixture of verbal threat and actual violence.

Under duress, and despite professional advice to the contrary, her will was altered entirely in favour of Petronella, and altered it had stayed.

Short of appealing to Petronella's sense of fair play, something the lawyer doubted would prove fruitful, there was nothing to be done. He was sorry, he said, but those were the unpalatable facts.

It was on this sad and depressing note that the meeting broke up. In the unlikely event of movement, Joffrey would contact both Joy and Spender. Something might be salvaged he said, but more in a tone of hope than realistic expectation.

Poor Joy, thought Spender. The double whammy. Six months ago he had been sure that his old friend was assured of a healthy present and a comfortable future. Now it seemed that there was to be no share of Gladdies, no Old Master painting, no Canadian mineral wealth, only the uncertain prospect of a miserly dividend from a niggardly family trust.

Not even enough for central heating at Perou to make his visits more comfortable.

The pretty road back to Kirkstiel seemed long and bleak.

Chapter 39

It was not an overly merry Christmas shared by Joy and Mick that year in France.

It is harder to have been shown the kingdom and then have it dashed away than ever to have been told of it at all.

They had dared to dream, encouraged by the siren voices of officialdom. That the dream had proved mirage, was no fault of those same officials but that was of little comfort to vanished expectation.

True, there was now the prospect of some small money where there had been none before, but real centimes are dull compared to imaginary francs.

Also true that a new world of cousins and family had opened for Joy and her children. Yet what use is a mother you have never met and never will?

Joy found this the most unsettling aspect of the whole affair. Mrs Turnbull was her mother, always had been, but now was apparently not.

Matthew though, was comforting. Someone real whom she had known and loved.

By the New Year these sad musings had been put away. Nothing had really changed, Joy decided.

There were still sheep to be fed and pictures to be painted. The world still turned and the last few months were nothing but a slightly mad interval. Better to forget Scottish silver or London gold. Love was the crucial thing and Mrs. Turnbull had given all she could. If she had owned anything else, she would have given that as well.

The frantic barking of the dogs heralded the arrival of the post van.

There was the usual heap of post Christmas mail. Late cards, thank you letters, publicity for the coming sales and festive bills.

She sighed, made coffee for them both and sat down with her husband to sift through the pile.

215

They opened the human correspondence first, then turned to the official. Among the latter Joy recognised Joffrey's hand on a stiff brown envelope. She opened it to find a further envelope, still sealed, and a covering letter.

'Dear Joy,' she read. 'I hope this finds you well. The enclosed came to me for onward forwarding. Evidently your whereabouts remain something of a secret. I took the liberty of making enquiries with the senders: their address is on the reverse of the envelope. There is no mistake, you are the intended recipient. Another lawyer I'm afraid.

When you have digested the contents please let me know if I can be of any help.

With kind regards to you both. John M Joffrey.'

Mystified, Joy took a knife and slipped the envelope open. Inside was a letter and four neatly stapled sheets of paper.

They were headed. *'Last Will and Testament of Arthur Wilfred Turnbull Esq.'*

She turned to the letter.

Dear Miss Turnbull,

My firm acts as executor for the estate of our late client, Mr Arthur Wilfred Turnbull.

Being unmarried and having no other issue, Mr Turnbull drew his will in favour of his only sister, Mrs Margaret Turnbull or in case of her demise, her child, Miss Joy Turnbull.

As you will observe from the date on the accompanying document, it has taken us some time to trace you.

To summarise, Mr. Turnbull's assets amount, in the main, to the following:

one house, various agricultural buildings, two traditional barns and some four hundred acres of Grade Two arable land.

This all situated in the county of Essex between the village of Stansted and the airport of that name.

Precise details attached.

In the period since your uncle's demise, we have been approached by several agencies in respect of his property.

These include a hotel chain, an international supermarket company and the airport authorities themselves.

I think that you will find their proposals interesting. Indeed there is something of a bidding round developing. The latest figures are attached below.

I should therefore be grateful if you would give this matter your prompt attention.

My firm will, of course, be happy to help with any technical advice or wealth counselling that you may require.

Yours sincerely,

Edward Cottrell. FRICS.

11 254 1010

2014

Lightning Source UK Ltd.
Milton Keynes·UK
UKOW05f0801211114

241908UK00001B/20/P